Unforgettable

CHERYL BARTON

Stand Alone Romance
Snowbound
Cupid's Arrow
One Wish
His Halloween Promise
Holly for Christmas
A Better Man
Bossy
Un-Break My Heart
Love on Top
Take a Knee
Love at First Sight
My First Love
Black Love
A Younger Man
The Lake House
True Lies or True Love
When I Think of You
*Baby, Come Back
(preorder, January 2021)
*Seize the Moment
(March 2021)
*His Holiday Wife
(February 2021)

Inspirational
Down, But Not Out: Breaking Chains
She Said No
Rescue Me
Release Me
*Restore Me

Unforgettable

Baltimorean Reagan Kelly was expecting an uneventful weekend in New York City visiting her sister between Thanksgiving and Christmas. Though in the holiday spirit, the last thing she thought she'd find on a cold, wintery night was a chance at romance.

Two days in New York City for business and a chance to see his best friend was all Crime Novelist, Keith Jackson had time for, or so he thought. He soon found time to extend his stay when the chance of a lifetime to spend four incredible days with the most beautiful woman he'd ever encountered landed at his feet.

An unforgettable weekend is one thing, but can that weekend turn into a lifetime of unconditional love for Reagan and Keith, two self-professed workaholics, who didn't have a reason to slow down and smell the roses until now?

Prologue

Reagan Kelly rushed through Baltimore/Washington International Thurgood Marshall Airport hoping that she would be able to escape an encounter with the last person on earth she wanted to see; her ex-boyfriend, Colin Evers, a man she once thought she'd one day share a last name with. The fact that he dumped her on the night of an important celebration of a career accomplishment in her life hadn't just embarrassed her when she thought she would be getting an engagement ring, but disappointed her when she discovered the reality was that he saw her more as a competitor than as a lifelong mate.

The heels of her Goldy Tall leather boots in Cognac, the closest to her favorite color, burnt orange, clicked loudly as she moved swiftly. The click, clack noise sounded like bombs dropping in her ears as the evidence of her rushing echoed all around her. People stared in her direction as if her movement bothered them. She saw faces leering at her with looks of wonder as to why she was moving expeditiously since she wasn't heading to catch a flight, but heading out of the airport. She ignored them and without caring what anyone thought, she kept it moving.

Seeing Colin after five years was a shock to her system and she could only hope that though she'd seen him as clear as day as she hurried to pick up her luggage, that he hadn't seen her, allowing her time to escape facing him as the mortifying events of their last encounter played in her head. She could still hear him telling her that he wanted a woman who would be happy just being his wife, taking care of his home and raising their children and not a woman as ambitious and definitely not more ambitious in the business world than him. His words were an insult to everything she'd worked hard for and still, even the thought of the conversation cut through her like a knife.

She was happy the moment she reached the luggage belt just as bags in all shapes and colors started careening down, falling in all directions. Pulling the faux-fur collar of her full-length leather coat, which matched the color of boots, up around her face as much as possible, she tapped the sole of one of her boots nervously on the epoxy floors of the airport terminal, trying to mentally persuade her luggage to fall quicker to allow for a dignified retreat. What was Colin doing back in Baltimore? Was he coming or going? She didn't know and she didn't care. She kept her mind on the prize, which was getting to her car in the long-term parking lot.

Excitement zipped through her when she saw her red and black single piece of luggage fall to the baggage carousel. Pulling her favorite Louis Vuitton Monogrammed Canvas purse close to her side, she moved quickly to the belt and just as she was about to grab the handle, another hand reached for it and lifted it for her and out of her reach.

"Let me, Reagan Kelly. It is still Reagan Kelly, right?"

She cringed. She knew that voice and without thinking about what she was doing, she inhaled deeply, knowing she would get a whiff of his favorite cologne, *Aventus* by Creed. The moment the aroma tickled her nostrils, their entire relationship flashed through her mind and she shivered, not out of desire, but out of disenchantment.

The fact that he had to stress the point that he knew she hadn't married by now was disconcerting on so many levels, but she stood tall, turned to him and smiled. The minute her eyes landed on his handsome face and the chiseled features she remembered so well that all women found magnetic, she wished she'd never looked his way.

"Yes, it's still Reagan Kelly. How are you Colin?"

"I'm married with two beautiful children. Did you hear that I'm married to the former Miss Texas?" he exclaimed with more excitement than was needed for the conversation.

Reagan shook off the extra information he provided without her asking, but she played along. She was feeling quite petty today.

"Oh, she wasn't a high achiever, not reaching Miss America status or did you finally meet a woman who would give up her dreams just so that she could be called Mrs. Evers?"

Not realizing until after she'd spoken, Reagan noticed that each word felt like she had spit them out in disgust.

"Still hating I see."

His smirk made her want to slap him, but she didn't – he never was and still isn't worth it.

When she tried to get her bag from his hands, she huffed when he started walking toward the exit as if he was using his mind to summon her to follow. She didn't have a choice; he still had her bag.

"I can carry my bag from here. Thanks for picking it up for me."

"No problem. I take it you're coming from some business trip for the bank, Miss Senior Vice President. Yes, I heard about the promotion and I guess congratulations are in order. You got what you wanted, but it's easy when your father owns the bank where you work."

Reagan turned her head and looked up at him as they stepped outside into the cold November air. Every ounce of will power was in use as she resisted the desire to remind him that her achievement, no matter how she got it, still outweighed any he has made. Just as he'd kept track of her life, she was well aware of his and she knew he needed to still keep hope alive that he'd reach her level one day.

"I worked hard for it," she proudly boasted.

"I'm sure you did. Still no time for fun, huh? I saw your sister and some of your friends earlier this month when I was flying into BWI for a meeting outside of Washington, D.C. I understand they were going on a girl's trip and when I asked her about you, why was I not surprised that you weren't with them, instead, choosing to be off on a business trip? Same old Reagan, huh? You still can't figure out how to have fun? All business and no play?"

Reagan formed her mouth with another petty comment about how she loved her life, but she didn't. She didn't need to explain anything to a man who led her to believe that they had a future together, only to toss her aside when she got the job that he was sidling up to her for two years, thinking he would get instead.

Exhaling, she found herself rising above and this time reaching for her luggage, she was able to get it from him and turned to walk away.

"Never a pleasure, Colin," she yelled over her shoulder as she walked away from him.

"Enjoy your, no fun at all having, next business trip, single boss lady; or not!"

His parting words unnerved her, but she wouldn't

dare let him see it on her face.

Ignoring him, she headed for her car and home to get a shower to wash off their encounter. Why did he have to remind her of how her life consisted of work, work, work and not much else? She didn't even have to tell him that was the case; he already knew.

1

After fuming for two long weeks and her anger not diminishing, Reagan decided now was a good time to finally return one of her sister's phone calls, though she knew Renee, the oldest of her sisters would play the victim as if irritation at her would be unwarranted.

After getting up at four in the morning to workout in her home gym, today had to be the day in order for her to move beyond her recent embarrassment, the result of running into her ex-boyfriend two weeks ago at the airport. Her sister will have an excuse that she'll use to try and smooth over the situation, but she wasn't planning on letting her off the hook.

After her workout, she rushed to get dressed and head to the office, all while focusing on how empty Colin made her life seem. The unexpected interaction took less than five minutes but it seemed like a lifetime. She was still bitter after letting him get to her, but never bitter over the end of their relationship. She was happy to get out of what she now knew was a toxic, one-way situation. Still, his smugness pissed her off and therefore, causing her to be livid at her sister for not giving her a heads-up.

Though it was earlier than when she would usually call Renee, she dialed her and impatiently tapped her freshly manicured fingernails on her car's steering wheel as she sat in her assigned parking space in the underground garage of the building where she worked. The second she heard Renee's voice, she barely gave her time for her usual chipper greeting.

"Why wouldn't you tell me you saw Colin Evers and why would you tell him you were going on a fun trip and that I was on a business trip which is why I couldn't join you?" she rattled off in a rant.

Her anger was filled with two weeks of fury that she had been left feeling vulnerable, though she held herself together well under the weight of his judgement. She couldn't seem to shake the sarcasm behind every word that left his mouth.

"Reagan, what are you talking about and why are you screaming at me before I've had even one cup of coffee? It's too early for drama. Calm down and speak without screaming or I'm going to hang up on you," Renee replied calmly.

Reagan started to dig into her again with harsher words, but exhaled and now letting her anger go, she knew Renee was right – it was too early in the morning to be this upset. It had taken her so long to call her sister and she'd been seething the entire time. She tried forgetting about Colin, but every time she picked up a work folder or read a work email, she heard his remark about her still not knowing how to have fun. The *nerve!* He'd used those same words when he'd broken up with her.

"I'm sorry, Sissy, but he got under my skin," she finally said in a more tranquil tone.

"Who did? Colin? Where did you see him?"

Reagan had been filled with so much anxiety that now, with her body relaxing, she was able to explain without yelling.

"At the airport when I came back from the business trips I took to Texas and then to Chicago."

"Oh, the trip you took for daddy because he was too busy having fun while you slaved away at work, bouncing from state to state doing his bidding for him, pretty much every hour of the day? That one?" Renee asked with reproach.

Reagan started to retort but decided to let her snide remark slip away.

"Not you too. I was doing my *job*. Why is that such a bad thing?" she asked.

"Reagan, it's not a bad thing, but even I've said you don't spend enough time having fun. You're thirty-two years old and your every waking hour is spent thinking about and doing work for the bank. You do realize you can have your career and every now and then, take a girl's trip to let your hair down?

What did Colin say, exactly?"

"He said he saw you when you and the girls were going on that girl's trip a few weeks back. He made a sly remark about me still being all about work and no fun. I was so pissed that I didn't know what to say. He also shared, without me asking, that he was married with some kids, like I care," she huffed.

"You do care or you wouldn't be bothered. Let it go. He was and still is a jerk. He's not memorable so I didn't remember that I ran into him and I assumed it wouldn't be a big deal since it's been years since you've talked to him. Why would I bring him up when I know the thought of him turns you into the terrible side of yourself? I hate to remind you of this, but he pretty much admitted he was with you in hopes of landing a position at the bank, thinking daddy was going to give him the junior vice president position over you and anyone else. He's just bitter it went to you, as if the situation was going to turn out any other kind of way. You were and still are too good for him anyway. If this is why you have been avoiding my calls and texts for two weeks, do better. You let some creep make you angry at me, your favorite sister. Don't tell Jen I said that. Now, I need to give my husband a little something, something to start his day and get some coffee before my kids get up and need all of my attention before school. Are you home or at work?"

"I'm in the garage at the bank. I just pulled into my parking spot."

"Reagan, let it go. You are who you are. What you had with Colin was never meant to be and try not to let him get to you. None of us liked him and there were times when I questioned how much you liked him. The next time I see him, I'll kick him in the balls, just because, and I'll remind him to never mess with my baby sister again. How's that?" Renee asked.

Between Renee's laughter on the other end and the visual image of Colin doubling over in pain, she couldn't help but laugh and smile herself.

"Kick him twice and then I'll be happy!" Reagan laughed out loud. "Sorry I yelled at you this early in the morning. I have a crazy day ahead of me and I poured my frustration out on you."

"You know you can always do that, but try and do it after eleven or twelve on any given day, after coffee and my morning of getting freaky with Fred!"

"Renee Boston, you are just *nasty*! Ugh! Bye."

Reagan disconnected the call and sat with her hands resting on the steering wheel, knowing she was behind schedule for her first meeting of the day, but reluctant to move. For a few moments, she'd been focused on her past and now came time for her to focus on the day ahead and the idea of it had her sitting without making an honest attempt to get out of her car.

She was the queen of stalling and she was mastering the technique as she looked at the concrete wall ahead of her. Rubbing her hands across the soft red leather seats of her shiny, new black Tesla, her hesitation with going to work this morning was replaced with appreciation of the benefits of being a bank senior vice president, even if that bank was owned by her father, Ernest Kelly.

American Harbor Bank and Trust, headquartered out of Baltimore, Maryland with nationwide branches was one of the largest African American owned banks in the country. Her father worked hard for years as the owner and major stakeholder to take the bank to a level that surpassed any expectations his own father, Edward Kelly had before he passed away from a heart attack, leaving the bank to his son to keep the Kelly name on people's lips for centuries to come.

She loved the day she graduated with her degree in finance from Hampton University, where she'd first met Colin. After their breakup, she focused on going to school part-time to get her doctorate degree and tired not to look back to what could have been.

Some may see her elevation to Senior Vice President of Operations and Expansion over the twenty east coast branches as one given to her because of who her father was, but she knew that the promotion a year ago came as a result of her education and hard work. From where she sat, her life could be admired because of what she has achieved, but no one knew the real story of how her happiness was fleeting with each given day because even before seeing Colin and having to deal with him, she had already begun to feel unfulfilled; something she'd kept to herself.

Nothing in her life was taken for granted, but it wasn't all peaches and cream. The part she disliked awaited her several floors up where she worked some ten to twelve hours a day, barely getting a break to enjoy her new car more than the ride into the office and then back to her new home in Harford County, Maryland, an area known for good, quiet living, a big difference from the condominium she had been living in that made her feel claustrophobic. She needed that quietness after work days that consisted of one meeting after another or one business trip after the other, bringing an insurmountable amount of exhaustion into her life. How could she have not realized how utterly tiresome her life was and that wasn't just some days, it was every day? She couldn't even remember the last time she'd taken a real vacation. Her father was all about business and he expected to see her in the office as much as he was with constant reminders that he was preparing her to one day take over for him.

She woke up feeling some kind of way about her life and it wasn't something that made her smile, especially after Colin's words haunted her again and again. She had her nice house, car and funds in the bank, which wasn't something to throw a stick at knowing someone would love having even a small portion of what she has acquired. Something only she knew was that she would give it up for what was missing from her life – love and happiness with a man who loved and appreciated her for who she was; workaholic and all. She still had plenty of time to get both, but the pressures of where her father wanted her career to go had her so focused on work that having any kind of life escaped her.

Knowing she had to get going, she reached for the door handle and then paused, choosing instead to lean forward, allowing her head to rest on the steering wheel. She really wasn't prepared for the schedule ahead of her and it was only Monday. Before she could clear her head and make the decision to get out as she did every morning, there was a tap on the window and the surprise presence shocked her right back up into an upright seated position. Moving her thick, natural flowing curls out of her eyes, she looked to her left to see who had disturbed her one moment of peace and to her chagrin, she saw Buster Gibbs, the one man who resented everything about her and any woman in a position of leadership over him. Perhaps, he should give up being called Buster and go with his given name, Brandon. Lowering the window when he didn't make a move to walk away, she turned her head up and gave him her usual fake smile.

"Well, well, well, is the new vice president sleeping at work? Looks like you've been caught slipping, but you and I both know it's not your first time slipping now, is it? Are you coming or going? I ask because I know that you don't have any kind of life other than this place, so I wouldn't put it past you to work on a Sunday well into Monday morning," he said.

Reagan exhaled coming face to face with another man she allowed to consistently get under her skin.

"Really, *Buster*?" she replied, stressing the two syllables of his name in a way that she knew he hated. "It's too early in the morning for your, *'I hate women so I'm going to be annoying'* kind of start to the day. I'm not slipping or sleeping and no, I did not work last night. I'm just getting here and about to make my way upstairs. What can I do for you?" she asked, but didn't really mean for him to respond. Knowing him, he would and in a way that she wouldn't like. Their daily nice-nasty kind of banter was getting old, especially when her thoughts lately about work were shaky.

"Me? I'm never like that," he replied facetiously

"Buster, you're like that every day. What's next, some kind of clever observation accompanied by your reminder that I'm in my position because my family owns the bank? Come on, hit me with your best shot and move on. It's been a year of this from you and at least once a week, you toss that out in a show to everyone that you're bitter that you're not in my position," she boldly countered.

Where was this woman when she ran into Colin? She needed this lethal tongue then.

"Hey, I don't do that and no one can say that it

would have been you if you weren't who you were or are. I'm just saying, it's what people are saying and I'm just not countering it."

"I can't with you today. Move so that I can open my car door," she stressed without patience for his usual antics.

Reagan grabbed her purse and her bag that contained too many electronic devices which she needed for work. She would love, just once, to be able to leave her house and leave everything except her cell phone behind; just once.

Stepping out, she started to walk away when she turned as Buster walked around her car, checking it out.

"Whew, the things a big promotion can provide. What are you doing with all of that money you're making? You don't travel, no husband, no kids, still no boyfriend either? Nice car. I bet this set you back a pretty penny, but that's just pocket change for you, huh?"

Walking away didn't mean she couldn't throw some shade his way.

"Buster, I see you in your expensive suits and shoes, you drive a Mercedes sports car, you throw parties with expensive food and drinks and you travel every chance you get, sharing your photos from every exotic island in the world, so I'm not the only person making money. Don't throw stones at material things because it's beneath you and don't touch my car," she sneered.

When he lifted both of his hands as if he were surrendering, she sucked her teeth and kept walking.

"Oh, who is being all bougie, rich and mighty now?"

"Whatever. I'll see you in the office," she said and tried to walk faster.

"What? And miss the opportunity to ride in the elevator with you? Not on your life. Say, I'm having a party this weekend. You should come and bring a date, if you do that sort of thing – man or woman – no judgement here."

"Do you wake up and go to bed judging? I'm busy this weekend," she lied. The last place she would be caught was at one of Buster's infamous parties with heavy drinking, barely dressed women, bumping, grinding and where she heard other paraphernalia could be found. She tried not to judge, but she wasn't interested in being his friend. Working with him was enough. She'd known him a lot of years, even before he started working at the bank a few years ago and she could honestly say, she's never liked him. She tolerated him, not because he worked at the bank, but because his family had a tie to hers.

"Really? What's the new VP got on her agenda for the weekend? Working around the clock? I hear you're being groomed to take over because your father is thinking about retiring in a few short years. Is that true or just rumor?" Buster asked.

Reagan tried to walk faster to get away from him, though her favorite pair of black, five-inch *Manolo Blahnik's* didn't make moving quicker an easy option.

"Stop listening to gossip," she blurted out.

She poked the elevator button again and again, even though she knew the action wouldn't make it come any faster.

"It's not gossip, and I'm thinking we could work together as a team and make this a win-win for us both."

Where was a good elevator when you needed one? She wanted out of this conversation, but with him, that wouldn't be possible.

"How can we do that?" she finally asked.

"You as bank president and me in your current position. We could put a rockin' team together with branches in all fifty states. Imagine that! A black-owned bank even in cities that couldn't imagine supporting it. The strong presence in the current market could only increase with us putting our heads together. Think about it."

Reagan was thinking of everything but the idea of them working that close together.

"I have enough to think about in my current position. I'm not working on plans for taking over in the future."

She wanted to say more, but the elevator door finally opened and quickly jetted to the lobby floor where it filled up with others, giving her what she hoped was a reprieve from him making a pitch for a job where there wasn't a vacancy. She moved as far to the left as she could and gave a sigh of relief when three people now stood between her and Buster.

The man worked her last nerve. He was thirty-five, handsome, good with money and ambitious, the last of the descriptions she was impressed with. For some reason, her being good with money came as a shock to him and she's heard him say that about other women too, as if women can't walk and talk at the same time. Buster lived in his head where men reigned and women existed. He was the kind of man who believed that women should be seen and not heard and should be in the background, leaning on his every word and making moves only with his support. She knew plenty of men like that and for that reason, she worked harder to make her own way. Women of today have tired of waiting for someone to bring the American dream into their lives. Like her, they hit the pavement just as hard as any man. It was sad that they were often not celebrated as much as their male counterparts, an experience she lives through every day.

Reagan took advantage of the crowded elevator, knowing that by the time it reached the top two floors where the executive offices for the bank were, she and Buster would again be in the elevator alone and he'll go back to torturing her, something that gave him great pleasure.

As the car moved from floor to floor, she prepared for the last person to exit and hoped that Buster would refrain from talking, allowing her to get out of the elevator without her hatred for him growing. As soon as the door closed, her silent wish went ungranted.

"My party this weekend is going to be lit. You can even come stag if that makes it easier. You know, you are a gorgeous woman and all that beauty is going to waste with you not having a man."

"Oh, what an appealing invitation. How are you still single after a quip like that?" she asked glibly.

"I haven't decided on the woman who will be lucky enough to win my heart. There are so many to choose from who want the job. For now, I enjoy spreading myself amongst as many lovely women as I can. Too bad you're all about business and have no real social life. You could have had your chance with me, but I prefer women I don't have to compete with – you know, those who don't feel they have to have as strong a backbone as me; no disrespect, seriously. There are some women who make a man feel like he has to compete with whose is bigger, if you know what I mean."

Reagan knew what he meant and she had a riposte all planned, knowing what was coming, but she didn't think Buster could stoop as low as he just did, not only insulting her, but insulting every woman on the planet who chooses to make a lane for herself.

She opened her mouth to respond and then closed it. What she was planning to say wasn't good enough.

Turning so that she was facing him full on, she chose her words carefully to make sure he took her response with him throughout the day, though she doubted he would even care.

"Men like you are the problem, Buster. See, you don't think a woman can have it all, a high-profile, high-paying job, a man and a life, but she can. Just because you don't have an in to every part of my life doesn't mean I don't have one. I feel sorry for any woman you decide to 'choose', and I use that term loosely because when you do come across that woman, I'd like to chat with her about her self-esteem. You don't have to talk down to women to make yourself look big, tall and manly. I never talk down to you and I can't, for the *life* of me, understand why you feel the need to come for me every chance you get. I got it, you've known me for a long time, prior to us working together, so you think we're close enough that you can treat me any kind of way. You can't! Women are more than the floosies I see you flaunt out and about – most are only about their bodies and nothing else. Lucky for me, I have beauty and brains and when I decide that there is a man who appreciates me, all of me and it never has or will be you, he will love *all* that he and I can be together and not just who he can conquer and keep in place. That's not a relationship. My last warning to you is, back off, tone it down, pull it back or the woman that *I AM* and the position that *I AM* in will whip out my balls, throw them over my shoulder and make sure that your view of them will always be from behind me. Now, if you'll excuse me, as senior vice president, I have meetings to get to and instead of that report that you're working on that's due to me by Thursday, I expect it on my desk by the end of day today. Just in case, you end up working late to get it finished, make sure you're not found asleep in your car in the garage in the morning. I'd hate to assume it's because you don't have a life other than this place. If you ever try to disrespect me or any other woman in this company, again, I'll make sure you are looking for another job. Oh, and just in case you are wondering, that was my response to let you know that *mine* are bigger. You don't want this fight with me. I like having a mind of my own, a career I worked hard for and a life that's none of your business. Anything else I can help you with this morning, *Buster*?" she asked harshly.

When the slick smirk left his face and he lifted his hands in surrender again, she finally exhaled and walked away. She had more she wanted to say which had been festering inside of her, but she held back. They were once cordial when they were both junior executives until she moved up and he found the need to demean her because he thought he could. Buster was where he was at the bank because of her father's choosing. He is the son of a friend from her father's college days, but not even for her father would she continue to take mess from Buster who thought women were beneath him.

"He needed to hear that one! He came for the wrong one!"

Reagan turned her head as she heard Malcolm, another of the bank's junior associates, speak and give her a head nod. Not only had the women at the bank had enough of him, but so did the men.

"Yeah, he did!" she declared as she walked past her assistant, Sherry and into her office. She was sick and tired of men like him and like Colin. All women deserved better.

2

"Invite her and see what happens."

"She's not going to come. My sister is the biggest workaholic I know."

"Baby, if you don't invite her, you'll never know. You have said it time and time again that Reagan never has any fun. Didn't you say she called you hollering at you because some old boyfriend told her the same thing? You have a chance to have a hand in turning that around and you're second-guessing yourself. This was your idea and as your husband and the love of your life, I am here to support you."

Renee looked lovingly across the kitchen table at her husband Frederick Boston as they, once again, talked about how worried she was about the direction Reagan's life was going in. She could relate and wanted more for her.

"She's going to give me another excuse just as she always does. She hasn't been to New York since we moved into the new condo. Our kids only know her because of video chatting. When we all went through the pandemic and all we could do was video chat was one thing, but the pandemic has been alleviated by the current administration and we can get back together again. Did I tell you that at the last minute, she cancelled on joining me, Jennifer and some of our friends for the girl's holiday trip to the Poconos a few weeks back? It was the Halloween trip of trips and she ghosted us. Remember that trip? It had been planned for almost a year since most of us have children and had to plan around school and making sure the kids were taken care of before we took a four-day trip. I was so mad at her. We were already at the airport when she called to tell me she couldn't make it because of some work thing. That was when I ran into Colin, here in New York at the airport and she couldn't find time to get away, not to mention that she also cancelled on the island getaway last summer. It was our time to celebrate. I keep trying to get her to have fun and she fights me all the way."

Renee got up and leaned back against the kitchen counter with a hot cup of coffee in her hands allowing it to take off the morning chill she always felt. As she watched Fred, her husband of eight years eagerly chow down on two buttermilk pancakes and turkey bacon while she contemplated her next move with her sister, she delighted at the thought of how happy she was choosing the life she wanted and not the one someone else wanted for her. She wasn't trying to plan out Reagan's life either, but she knew when her sisters were unhappy, especially Reagan. Their sister, Jennifer, who lived in Chicago with her husband, Jonathan Bryant and son, Josiah was a little harder to read, but Reagan was transparent with her emotions living on the inside and all over her face. Reagan often struggled with getting out of her own way. She had to do something since it didn't appear Reagan would make moves to be happier.

"Then invite her to come here for a visit this weekend. It's a short train ride from Baltimore to New York and it's only four days. You told me how much she loves Jill Scott and this concert is the perfect opportunity to get her away from the office."

"I know. She's been crazy busy since getting that promotion over a year ago. My father overworks her and she just goes along with it."

"Your sister is more like him than you or Jen are. She's always been driven to get his approval. She's the youngest and the only one of his girls that he could get to follow in his footsteps."

Renee shook her head in agreement. She found herself with the same thought all the time.

"I wanted a life outside of the office. We all went to college, taking up finance just to make him happy. He has drilled in each of us since birth that we were to one day take over running the bank. He should have had more children and maybe he would have gotten the son he always regretted not having."

Renee knew what was coming and she regretted the words the second they left her mouth.

"That's mean and you know it," Fred asserted.

"I know; I'm just angry. He's never made us think he wished we were boys. That was a horrible thing for me to say. I can't remember a time when my father didn't work seven days a week, around the clock. I'm surprised he and my mother found the time to make the three of us. He's turned my sister into a mini him and I hate it."

"Why does she feel so obligated to your father?" Fred asked.

Renee had enough background to fill hours of conversing on that topic, but she only had about another hour before the kids got up for school. She decided to give Fred the abbreviated version.

"She's always been the sister who was closest to him and the only one of us not willing to defy his every wish for our lives. I love my father, but I didn't want a life that was solely devoted to the bank. Reagan played sports where me and Jen refused. You know I still hate sports. She could dance at a ballet recital one minute and then be on the basketball court playing a strong guard the next. For all that she did to get his attention growing up, he never showed up for anything on time – most times not at all, but that didn't stop her from doing more to please him. She even entered a golf tournament as his partner though she hates the sport. He has worked hard to keep the bank in the family, keeping himself as the primary stakeholder in ownership. Being that driven took him away from us as we grew up and it's why my mother eventually divorced him. I hate what he's done to Reagan, turning her into the new him."

"Baby, that's why as her oldest sister, if you want to do something about it, now is the time. I told you why it has to be this weekend. We may not get this chance again. Who can give up being in New York for a weekend of shows, concerts, shopping and family? The town is decorated for Christmas and we know how magical that can be. She missed the family Thanksgiving with us last week, so play on her guilt over that. You know she'll cave under pressure from you."

"I know and you're right. She's been promising me that she would visit and not once has she kept her promise. I don't like seeing her stressed out all the time."

Renee sipped her coffee and turned with her back to Fred as she thought. She had to do something or watch precious years for Reagan slip away. She leaned back when Fred came up behind her and held her around the waste, peppering her ear and neck with kisses, allowing her to relax and think clearer.

"I don't like to see you stressed out about someone else's life. Reagan is blessed to have you and Jennifer and I respect that you want to see her life go in a different direction, but for starters, she has to be open to having more in her life than just work and also, if nothing comes out of this weekend, if she agrees to come, you have to promise me that you won't continue to worry about her."

Renee started to agree and then pulled her lie back. She was *never* going to stop looking out for Reagan, even for her love life.

"Fred, when was the last time you heard me say that I talked to her and she had been out on a date with anyone? I want more for my baby sister. I know she wants her own family and the reason she doesn't visit me or Jen, Jonathan and Josiah is because she is jealous of the lives we have and that's not me making an assumption. She literally told me that, and more than once. When I asked her why she would settle for a life that didn't mirror what she wanted for herself, she said that me and Jen abandoned our dad by not working as a family at the bank and how disappointed he was when we decided to follow our own dreams and not his dream for us. I loved working there, but the positions he wanted us in would secure a life of work and not much else. We each have trust funds left to us by our grandfather, so it's not about the money and you know I'm not a clout chaser, so it's not that either. I just wanted to do me. I'm a true believer that a woman can have it all, but I remember what it felt like never having my dad around because he was so busy at the bank and I didn't want that for me. I wanted a career, the one of my choosing and I wanted to make sure I gave my children equal time. My mother didn't work outside the home and that made it easy for her to cater to us, but I wanted different and that different didn't turn out to be the bank," she explained.

She and Fred had talked many times over the years about her family life, but she couldn't remember ever telling him how abandoned she felt when it came to their father.

"What if that's really what Reagan wants but she just isn't telling you that?"

Renee turned and faced Fred, this time wrapping her arms around him, enjoying their closeness.

"I know my sister; I know both of my sisters. We have always been close and that didn't change when I moved to New York or when Jen moved to Chicago. When I met you, I was on the same path that Reagan is on right now. Do you remember that day?" she asked.

When Fred smiled as he thought back on that day, she beamed knowing how much fate had a hand in their meeting that day, one of the best days of her life, though she didn't know it immediately.

"What kind of husband would I be if I didn't remember the day that I met you? You were rushing to a meeting at the bank in Baltimore and you almost ran me down at the corner of Charles and Light Street, pretty much running a red light and growling at me like I was in the wrong. You threw the finger up at me as you sped forward and like I've always said, though you couldn't see me, I smiled as you drove away. I could see your head moving back and forth, no doubt you were cursing me out. A few hours later, you sat across the table from me completely stunned when I reminded you of who I was as your father and his associates convinced me to move my software company's business to his bank. There was no way I would have forgotten the beauty behind the wheel. After the meeting, you apologized profusely as we rode in the elevator down to the lobby and I ate all your loveliness up!" Fred gloated.

"My father made me apologize to you when I told him what happened. After you left, he asked me what was going on, sensing my discomfort throughout the presentation to you. I was going to apologize anyway, but he beat me to it with an immediate request to do so and suggested I ride down with you to make sure what happened didn't interfere with his ability to do work with your company. The bank had been trying to get your business to switch to the bank for a few years."

When Fred nuzzled her neck and kissed her on the precise spot he knew drove her wild, she giggled like a school girl, encouraging him on.

"Best decision of my life because not only did I make the switch, but getting that contract to upgrade the bank's software for all the main offices and branches was the extra step-up I needed to really expand the company. He was the connection to a lot of the business contracts my company still has today. I appreciate your father for that, but mostly, I appreciate his beautiful daughter who married me, making me the happiest man alive with two kids who make my world go around."

"Ditto on that!" Renee chimed.

When Fred kissed her softly on the lips, she moaned her pleasure against his perfect pair.

"What I remember the most about that day was that you didn't slap me when I kissed you before the elevator reached the lobby," Fred said.

The deep, sexy tone of his voice had her remembering how grateful she was for that day and the kiss he laid on her without asking.

"That's because I was stunned by lust. I'd never been kissed so passionately before. I was seeing stars and rockets and was mad when the elevator stopped and you pulled away," she admitted.

"I told you that day that if you joined me for dinner later, I would share with you how wonderful a life we were going to have one day as husband and wife and neither of us ever looked back. I've never been happier in my life until the day you accepted my ring and my proposal," he said.

"Each and every day is more perfect than the last. That's what I want for Reagan. She deserves that and I say that because I know she wants it. I'm not wanting something for her that I don't know whether she wants it for herself or not; trust me, I do. She needs a man who will take her as she is and also show her that there is more to life that can be balanced with her dreams. She seems to meet men who want her to be someone different than who she is in order for them to want her. She's smart, beautiful, ambitious and has a heart of platinum! With the right man who would appreciate her, the sky would be the limit on how good life could be, personally and professionally. She needs a man just like you," she admitted.

"Baby, that's because you took the time to smell the roses. I never wanted to take you away from your job at the bank or any position you wanted to have or any goal you wanted to reach. I will always be by your side, supporting you in everything. I have always told you that you can have any and everything you want in life and I would be your number one supporter. If you needed me to scrub office floors or find a way to build you a building, I would move heaven and hell to do it because I love you enough to watch you get everything out of life you desire, especially me."

When his last words came with a deeper kiss, she melted in his arms. She looked into his eyes and saw the love he showed to her every single day.

"I know. You said if I wanted to continue to work at the bank, that you would move to Baltimore because you could run your software company from anywhere in the United States and that wherever I was, is where you wanted to be. I wanted our life more than I wanted the rise to the top. I know I could have had both, but I wanted more time loving you and our kids and enjoying the life we have built here in New York. My dream of owning my own flower shop came to life because of the plans we made together. I have three locations in New York and that's because we saw what we could build together. I could have chosen work and business first, but I chose that second and chose love first. Thankfully, they came together with you."

"Jennifer followed her heart as well. Not that her heart, like yours, couldn't have been at the bank, but you wanted more; you both wanted it all and you showed you could have it. She's in Chicago about to launch her own talk show in the old studio that Oprah once owned. She's doing big things in business and still managed to carve out a personal life with a husband and son and you said they are planning on having at least one more."

"I need Reagan to see that she can have the life she dreams of. When I talk to her and I ask her about her dating life, she always reverts back to a conversation about the bank as if to hide the fact that she doesn't know how to slow down and smell the roses."

"Babe, then this weekend is perfect. You said yourself that she hasn't even taken a few days off since she got that promotion a year or so ago and the weekend comes with us putting her up at the Marriott

Marquis, your favorite hotel here in the city so that the kids wouldn't bother or nag her all weekend. The two of you could have the time of your lives and the kids and I can do some fun activities after the concert on Friday night. Besides, you need to tell her that your mother is getting remarried. I know Reagan is still bitter that she left your father and moved on, but everyone deserves their own brand of happiness, especially your mother."

Renee still struggled with Reagan being the only one of them that didn't know their mother was engaged to marry another man.

"Yes, especially my mother. She waited forty years for my father to find time for them to enjoy the fruits of his labor and he never followed through on any of his promises to her. She got tired of waiting for a life that wasn't about the bank. Each time he opened more branches and promised that he would take his money, sell the bank and enjoy empty nesting with her, he gave her another excuse. She waited and waited a long time to have him back and she never got that. He thought throwing money, houses, boats, cars, trips for her and her friends and expensive jewelry would make her happy, but all she ever wanted was him, especially after us girls all grew up. She was lonely in that big beautiful house. When she left him, he blamed her and tried to make us think it was her fault. Reagan fell for it, but Jen and I knew better. I love my father, but my mother was no longer happy and she deserved the life she wanted. She has found that with Walter and I couldn't be happier for her."

"Why hasn't she told Reagan about getting engaged?" Fred asked.

"Reagan is daddy's baby – she's a daddy's girl and my mother didn't know how Reagan would take the news, so I agreed to break it to her."

"Good. It's all planned out and depending on what she's open to, this weekend will be one for the books that we can all look back on and say we remember when and that we had a hand in it."

"I still don't know. Maybe she'll think I'm overstepping."

"Now, you know that's not anything new."

Renee nibbled nervously on her bottom lip.

"What will he think? He has become one of your best friends again, like you were back in college. Even the years where you were both chasing your dreams and lost contact, he easily came back into your life like the two of you never missed a beat. Won't he be pissed that you're doing this behind his back?" she asked.

"I'm not worried about him and you shouldn't be either. You want to show your sister a different side of life and we both think that this is a perfect situation and even if it doesn't work out like we hope, you can still show her a great weekend. I want to see you happy and to do that, you need to stop worrying about your sister. I have a way to help with that, I hope, but you have to do your part and convince her that the bank can survive without her being there for four days."

Fred was right and she knew it. No need for doubt. If Reagan couldn't find a way to help herself, she had a big sister who was willing to step in and do that for her, even uninvited.

"I'll do it. You're sure it's a good idea? I mean, we don't make it a habit of budding into other's lives," she said.

She was already feeling good about what could happen. She was perfect; he was perfect and together, they would be better than perfect, if there was such a thing.

"It will all be fine," Fred assured her.

"You're going to be late for your early morning meeting at the office, which is why I got up early to make you pancakes. Elijah and Amaya will be up in an hour. Don't you have a company to run and meetings to get to? My manager is opening the flower shop today, so I was planning on going in late after stopping by the other two shops and meeting with the staff in person at each. You can't be late," she said.

Renee sighed with pleasure the moment Fred moved closer to her and she could feel him and boy, could she feel him. She reached down between them to show him that she could.

"When you touch me like this, not only can I be late, but I'm thinking of a better way to fill my morning after the kids are off to school and it's just you and me here, all alone, with nothing but time this morning."

"Your meeting?" she asked, not that she cared, but she played like she did. She cared more about the desire she saw on his face and heard in his voice than she did about a meeting he'd set up.

"Consider it cancelled. I'll get the kids up and ready for school. I'll drop them off and when I get back, I'd like for you to be naked in any room you choose. What do you say?" he suggested.

Renee leaned up on her toes, kissed him deeply while also giving him the answer to his question. When the kiss ended, she turned, wiggled her hips a little extra for his benefit and laughed out loud when he started clapping like he'd just won the lottery; in truth, they both had.

3

"Reagan? Reagan."

Coming awake, Reagan had to take a minute to focus on where she was. When she looked up, she saw the white of the ceiling of her office and to her left, standing over her was Sherry, her assistant. She jumped right up as if she hadn't been sleeping, shaking off the cloudy sleep that fogged her mind.

"What time is it? Am I late for a meeting?" she asked, standing and straightening the skirt of her black suit while the jacket that she'd finally taken off earlier in the day had fallen to the floor beside the navy leather three-seat sofa in her office where she moved to earlier to focus on reviewing a report, but had somehow fallen asleep.

"No and sit back down. You needed to find some sleep. Your schedule lately has been crazy. You haven't missed any meetings. I cancelled the last two of the day after I found you asleep after your noon meeting. I closed your door, turned out the light and told everyone that you'd gone home early."

"What? Home early? I bet no one believed you," she said, rubbing the sleep from her eyes. "How long have I been asleep?"

"Well, it's six in the evening and you've been asleep since around two."

Shocked, Reagan whipped her head around.

"You let me sleep for four hours? What did I miss?"

"Nothing."

"Sherry, don't play with me. I know I missed something. I had two other meetings today. How could you let me miss them?"

Reagan rushed into the adjoining bathroom, grabbed a washcloth to run water to wipe her face, hopefully to help her wake up.

"Slow down and calm down. Your father came looking for you and I told him that you had an appointment outside of the office and you would be going home afterward."

"That wasn't a good move. Someone will see that my car is still in the garage."

"Not after I made it clear that you took a car service so that you could look over reports and that you asked me to alert security that your car would be in the lot overnight so that they could keep an extra eye out for it. I have all the bases covered. You really need to learn to relax more. I couldn't dream of waking you when I saw how tired you were all day. Buster brought his report by about an hour ago. He wanted to leave it on your desk and I threatened him with bodily harm if he even touched your office door handle."

Reagan chuckled, turned and tilted her head sideways.

"You should have just done it without the warning."

"I wanted to, but that would have woken you up and I needed to keep the façade that you were gone. Besides, he's a snake and doesn't deserve the attention. I told him I would make sure you got it, even if I had to fax it before I left."

"Speaking of that, you're still here. Why haven't you left? It may not be late for me, but for you it is. At least one of us should have a life," she joked.

"Oh, don't worry about me. Leo is meeting me at the gym right here downtown at seven and then we're doing a late dinner. He's been really busy lately and because we love working out, when we get to do it together, it's a perfect date for me. As long as we can get our time in, I'm happy and he makes me happy. Would you like to go with me? He has several friends who join him on Mondays."

Reagan started to respond, but instead, walked past Sherry and over to her desk where she sat down. The moment she touched the keyboard to her computer, it came to life.

"No, I'm good. I'm going to take a look at Buster's report and also check over the financials for the new branch in Virginia Beach. You go ahead and have fun," she said.

"You need to get out more. Did you do anything special for Thanksgiving?" Sherry asked.

"No. I was going to take a trip to New York to see my sisters. Jen and her family were there for Thanksgiving and so was my mom. I was too busy and didn't feel like traveling. I thought I would enjoy a quiet dinner with my dad, you know, since he and my mom aren't together anymore, but then I found out that he'd taken a trip to the west coast to visit with some friends."

"He didn't even ask what you were doing?"

Reagan looked side-eyed at Sherry knowing that the answer to that question was obvious.

"I'm sure he thought I was going to New York, so he didn't inquire."

"That would be true if he hadn't asked you to take a meeting for him the day after Thanksgiving, meaning he knew you would be in town, most likely working."

"I know, but it was fine. I watched my neighbor's two daughters so that he and his wife could go check out a movie that evening. They actually sent a plate over to my house and it was all delicious. I did make a small dinner, but then I didn't have to eat it. I put on some kid movies and we popped popcorn."

"I bet you got up the next day and checked your work email. You have to do better than that and this. Look at you now, unable to resist pulling up something work related. Go home and get some more rest and if you change your mind about the gym and even joining us for a late dinner, you know where I'll be and how to reach me."

"Noted. Have fun and thanks for covering for me. I have to admit that the nap was needed. I was exhausted."

"You need a vacation."

"Maybe."

When she looked up at Sherry, she was shaking her head in disbelief. She was another person trying to convince her that she needed more in her life than work. That may be true, but expectations were high for her new position and she had to live up to them. Though Buster had brought it up earlier, she refused to acknowledge the truth in his statement that her father was planning to retire and his plan was for her to step into his shoes to keep the Kelly name alive in the banking business. She would one day be bank president and ready for the job. She could only do that by focusing on work and making sure she made her father proud. Her sisters had deserted him and the business, but she wouldn't.

"No maybe about it. I've been your assistant since you first took a leadership position after college and when you got this new position, you brought me along. I care about you and I see how hard you work. What I don't see is you smiling and coming to work with any salacious stories to tell me. One day, though. I'm counting on that one day. I'm heading out. Do you need anything before I leave?"

If only, Reagan thought. Yes, shoe could use a man as attentive as hers. Isn't that what every woman wanted? Every day, Sherry came to the office with a new story of something her man did for her or something they did together. Where she found the time for so much fun, Reagan didn't know, but she did admire it.

"No, I'm good. I'll see you in the morning and feel free to come in a little later than usual. I appreciate you staying late tonight and make sure you put the extra hours on the overtime sheet."

"You're so good to me. Goodnight, Reagan."

"Night," she responded and turned back to her computer. The main office line rang and she ignored it, but when the ringing stopped, she knew Sherry had answered it. "I thought you were leaving," she yelled to the outer office.

"It's your sister on the line."

"Which one?"

"Renee and she said she already knows you're here so answer the phone."

Reagan grumbled under the breath and picked up the line. They had already spoken earlier in the day.

"How did you know I would be here at the office?

You could have called my cell," she said.

"Girl, stop playing with me. You think I don't know my own sister? I knew you would still be there and probably looking over some report or financials or something. What you're not doing is heading out on a date or even just to get that booty waxed for a change. Speaking of, did you get the little gift I sent you? I forgot to mention it when we spoke this morning after you chewed me out."

Reagan could hear Renee laughing on the other end, while she wasn't laughing at all. Who sends someone a sex toy with a label on it calling it her 'boyfriend'?

"It wasn't funny. You should have bought one for yourself and not me."

"Why? I have the real thing here and trust me, it's bigger and better than any toy. Can you say the same thing? You're letting cobwebs grown on that thing. What a waste of those Brazilian waxes you love to get. You're too busy working to allow a man to play in it! I figured you could use a new toy because any you already have is probably all worn out and the batteries are no longer keeping it working for hours on end. Why are you in the office this late?" Renee asked.

"I was just leaving."

"Lies!" Renee shouted.

"Seriously, I was."

"Lies, again."

Reagan exhaled loudly. There was no need in

lying to Renee. She had a sixth-sense for that.

"The financials for the new bank came in and I wanted to look them over before the meeting tomorrow."

"I knew it. I bet you've looked at them a million times and you could read off the projections without even looking at the file. I really want you to do better than work, work, work all the time."

"You work all the time, so why are you sweating me?"

Reagan leaned back in her office chair and placed her tired feet up on her desk, settling in for another speech from her sister about all the things that were wrong with her life.

"I do not work all the time because I hired people to run things when I know I need some down time like this morning when Fred and I took the day off and spent it in bed until the kids got home from school. I got a chance to try out the new stripper pole we bought and let me tell you how erotic that thing can be in the bedroom!"

"Too much information!" Reagan slid in, trying to end the amount of details she knew Renee was about to throw her way.

"Whatever! Don't hate because it doesn't look good on you. I'm already looking for ways to take even more time off and I'm not sweating you. I want you to find a life outside of the office. Find a man and get you some. Let a man wine and dine you and then get you some. Let love into your life from a hot, sexy, sweaty man and get you some! In other words, *get you some!*" Renee yelled.

"Why are you so obsessed with my love life?"

"You mean the lack of one? I'm not obsessed with it. I've been where you are and I know what it did to me. I got out before I allowed work to consume me. I'm not saying walk away from the bank and daddy. I would never tell you to do that. I want to see you spend just as much time having fun as you do at work, and besides, I'm calling to collect."

"Collect? Collect what? I don't owe you anything."

"Oh, but you do, little sister. So far, you have cancelled out on me twice last year, twice this year, actually three times if you include Thanksgiving last week and now I'm collecting on that. I want you to come to New York this weekend."

Reagan put her feet back on the floor and though she heard the words, she couldn't believe her sister thought that she just had free weekends laying around waiting to be used.

"No can do. I have a lot going on and now is not the time to take off and definitely not for two days or three day in New York," she said.

"Not two days, more like four days. I've booked you a train ticket for early Friday morning with a return ticket for Monday evening. You can get the train either at the station near you in Perryville or the one at Penn Station. I also have you booked into the

Marriott Marquis with plans for the Jill Scott show on Friday night, mad shopping all weekend, dinner, a play on Saturday and anything else you want to do as long as it's not work related."

"Renee? Why would you do that without asking me first? Can you get your money back? If not, I'll cover the expense, but I can't make it. I wish you and Jen would stop doing that, making plans, paying for them without asking me and then making me feel bad about cancelling when you know how busy I get."

"Reagan Amaya Kelly – you will *NOT* cancel on me again. Enough is enough already. I haven't seen you in person in a year. The kids miss you and I even named my daughter after you, giving her your middle name. You're their godmother and you need to spend more time with them and with me. We're sisters and we have to do better."

"Well, you don't see Jen either. Are you harassing her like you harass me?"

"I don't have to. I saw her on the island trip over the summer, I saw her back in October for the Poconos girl's trip and she was in town for Thanksgiving with her whole family. Actually, a few other times this year besides those I mentioned. I let you get away with avoiding me through last year's pandemic, but with that not being a big issue anymore, there will be no more excuses. We invited you and you ghosted us, like you always do, but not this time. Don't even try it. Come again with bigger knives to throw!" Renee yelled and then laughed at her.

Reagan pouted and still, she couldn't get one up on her sister.

"Damn! How are the two of you finding time to do all this going on trips and stuff with jobs and families?"

"We do because it's important to stay connected. Did the pandemic not show you anything about appreciating time together? I want you to appreciate more than your work life. Fred finds the time because he knows how important it is that we make as much time for each other as we make for our businesses. He's actually here next to me asleep and the kids are in the family room watching a movie after dinner. I'm about to get them some dessert before bed."

Reagan looked at the clock above the sofa on her office wall.

"Sleep? Is he ill? Why is he asleep at six in the evening? He must be sick."

She felt stupid the minute the questions flew out of her mouth.

"No, just tired. He's in a sex-coma from what I put on him and this last quickie was all about what he needed. Those jaw exercises came in handy!" she boasted.

"Again, way too much information sharing."

"Again, whatever! I had to put a pillow over his face to keep him from screaming, bringing the kids rushing to try and get into the locked bedroom," Renee quipped.

"You and Fred are just nasty! Y'all do it all the time and all over the place. I'm jealous!"

"Don't be jealous; there is a man waiting on you to serve up something hot and nasty on him. I don't know why you're in a desert right now. Do I need to go back to all the ways you should be getting some?"

Reagan put her hand up to stop her as if Renee could see her doing it through the phone. She was right on one aspect; she didn't know why she wasn't getting more on the regular. Had work really been consuming her that much? She didn't have time to date or even get a booty call right now, though she would like nothing more. She wouldn't dare thank Renee for the sex toy which she already knew was going to get a good workout when she got home later. Thankfully, Amazon delivered batteries to her house or she would get a side-eye from people if she was always seen with a multi-pack of double-A batteries in her cart. The thought of that being all she had to fall back on made her sick of herself.

"Anyway, that's a no for this weekend. I'm sorry."

"Don't be sorry. Get your behind on that train. You need to exhale and I have the perfect weekend plans to help you do that. I haven't seen you in forever and I need to lay eyes on you. Either you come to New York or I'll call Jen and we're going to show up in Baltimore this weekend. You can either do this my way, the non-embarrassing way or you can do this the Jennifer Bryant way and you know how extra our middle sister can be. She told me about the last time she came to visit you and you wouldn't leave the office to have lunch with her. She whipped out her phone, put music on and did a table dance in your outer office, embarrassing the hell out of you. Don't make me do it. Don't make me call her because if I hang up without your promise that you'll be on that train on Friday, I'm booking tickets for me and Jen to Baltimore. Your choice."

That nightmare of a display from Jen was the highlight of everyone's day around the office, except hers. Even their father saw the humor in her dancing on top of a table like she was auditioning for *Dancing with the Stars*.

"But, but, I can't and you know it. You know what I'm up against. The bank is a few months from the launch of a new Virginia Beach branch and other acquisitions. Don't do this to me," Reagan pleaded.

"I don't care and I don't sympathize either. That office can do without you for a few days. Work it out and carve out a few days for your sister. Now, shall I expect you or should I put in that call to Jen? I think her table dancing skills have gotten worse. Maybe she can dance and I can sing and you know how bad I am at that. She's the only one of us with no real rhythm, but she'll hit you with her off-beat moves in a minute. I may even have to ask her to throw in her terrible

Michael Jackson moonwalk moves. You up for that or nah?"

Reagan weighed her options even while she could hear Renee on the other end of the phone counting backwards from ten.

"Fine. I'll be on the train on Friday. Send me the information. How early is early? Not too early, I hope. Let me get in at least one meeting on Friday morning."

"Nope. Your train leaves just before seven in the morning and you know to be there early. I planned for your opposition to my plans and I'm telling you, do not cancel on me. Do you hear me, Reagan? Do not cancel on me. I need to see my sister and remind her that she has a sister who loves her and wants what's best for her. You're going to have fun and you know you can't pass up a Jill Scott concert. She's your favorite artist. Guess what? DJ Dnice is the opening act and you love him. Remember during the pandemic how he brought peace to people's lives with the sound of music over the internet? They are bringing back that last concert with him and Jill Scott from twenty-twenty which was the highlight of my year before the world went to hell. Now that we're over that and life is good again, it's time we got back to spending some real time together. Fred has the kids the weekend so that you and I can have our sister time. I'll even stay at the hotel with you if you want, just don't let me down."

Reagan exhaled and after hearing the plea in her sister's voice, there was no way she was going to let her down. She remembered the pandemic and the havoc it wreaked on everyone lives. She needed to appreciate having a sister who loved her.

"I won't. I promise, I'll be on the train. Jill Scott, huh?" she asked, excitedly.

"Yes, and I have some really good seats. See you Friday and travel safe."

Reagan hung up the phone and leaned back in her chair. She wondered how she was going to manage being out of the office for four days. She already knew that her father would have twenty heart attacks if she even mentioned taking a few days off, but four would send him to the grave. Renee was right. She needed some time away from the office, even if it was only for a few days.

She smiled thinking about the fun she and Renee could have around New York and she would get a chance to hug on her family in person for the first time in a long time. She was ready.

4

Fred ended his last meeting of the day, leaving his best friend and new partner, Crime Novelist Keith Jackson and him in the conference room alone. Not only were they the best of friends, but they were celebrating being new partners in the development of three movies based on the popularity of Keith's latest crime and espionage novel series with all three still sitting at the top of the New York Times Bestsellers list. Truth be told, Keith had written sixteen novels and each one was a number one bestseller. He looked forward to collaborating on film productions now that they were officially launching a new production company that they'd been working on for the past year. The pandemic provided a lot of time to think through new ideas and this one was golden. With them both being financially successful, they were happy to collaborate on a new dream; one they'd had since their college days.

"Man, I'm glad you made it to New York for this

meeting. I'm always happy to video conference all the planning, but doing this with the entire team in the room was much more productive," Fred said.

"Bro, I've been waiting a long time to connect with you on making movies and we've been at this planning for over a year. With your telecommunications and multimedia background, we are breaking ground on something new that's going to take the world by storm."

"Sho' you're right. I know everyone expected you to sign on with a major network and studio to turn your books into movies. I'm glad we were able to connect and strategize our way to the top without the puppet strings telling us what we can and cannot do."

"We have to look out for each other and we have the talent to do what we need to do to make this venture a major one. I still remember our college days when we dreamed big of a moment like this and now it's actually happening. The time is right and together, we have the money to do this ourselves, starting with the creation of the production company. Having our money people, writers and producers here for the meeting is the start to something great and I'm looking forward to it," Keith said.

"How far did I set you back with your unpacking? I know you just moved to Baltimore where we plan to build the studio as well as shoot each movie between there and Washington, D.C. Had you even had the chance to unpack any boxes? How is the new condo?"

Fred asked.

He started out feeling bad about asking Keith to take a trip to New York a week after he'd moved to Baltimore, but staying on schedule was important and the fact that his friend had no issue with turning right back around after his flight from California to taking a quick, short flight to New York showed how much the project meant to him too.

"I love it. One of my favorite authors, Tom Clancy, owned a condo in the building where I live. I was able to convert two floors into one large, two-level condominium for myself and it overlooks the water. You'll have to see it when you come to Baltimore. I haven't unpacked anything. I have a company doing most of it and my sister is overseeing them and doing all of the decorating, so my place is in good hands until I get back home. My cars and my bike are on trailers from the west coast and should be there in another week. There's a lot going on, but all good things, brother."

"Where are you going to store them? Does your condo have that much parking? You have like two cars, a truck and a bike, right?"

"No, it doesn't. I also purchased a nice house between Baltimore and D.C. and I'll keep the cars there. While my oldest sister is in town from Los Angeles, she's going to work on decorating and furnishing it for me. It has four garages, plenty of space for all of my rides."

"That's good to hear. I don't want to be the cause of you not getting things done to get settled in."

"Hey, no sweat. Besides, I love New York and you promised me a vision of beauty that is Jill Scott. Are we still on for the show and dinner tomorrow night?"

Fred knew that this was the moment when he should come clean, but he couldn't get the words out. He'd been trying all morning after he picked Keith up from the airport for his two-day trip to New York. He tried to get him to stay longer, but the workaholic that was Keith, convincing him of more days in New York was like pulling teeth that weren't old and rotted; it wasn't happening. He was happy he agreed to stay the extra day and a half, not leaving until Saturday afternoon, the day after the concert.

Fred was wishing on a big star when it came to what he and Renee hoped for out of the weekend. If Keith knew what he had planned, it could be a short point of contention between them that would pass, but would still bring in a little shade. He decided to keep the additional plans around the show to himself and just let the chips fall wherever they will lay on the night of the concert.

"Of course, we are. Renee is looking forward to seeing you and right after the show, one of my friends, who owns a restaurant not far from where the show is, is expecting us for a dinner of steak and seafood. He's from Maryland, so you know his crab cakes are a wonder."

"Man, I can't wait for the show and dinner. One of the reasons I love Baltimore is because of my love for seafood and they have the best, not to mention steamed crabs. I plan to have them at least once a week," Keith bragged.

"I guess that means you're happy about moving back east after being on the west coast since we graduated from Howard," Fred said.

"Those were the days, weren't they? We got our life in on that campus and established our futures within those halls. I will forever be grateful for what Howard gave me, not just the education, but the focus and my career."

"Who knew that you would be the number one crime novelist in the country right now? I knew you had potential when we met in that creative writing class and you knocked every writing assignment out of the park. Your stories mesmerized us all, especially the professor. You won every writing contest back then and to see where you are fourteen years after graduate school is incredible. Who knew writing books could make a brother a millionaire several times over!" Fred exclaimed.

"That's a testament to some good books and even better financial planning, something I still owe to your wife. I know she's not in that business anymore, but when she offered to help me with investments and money principles, I've seen my investment portfolio increase beyond my dreams and now you and I are embarking on a lifelong dream of being in business together. This is going to be great. I'm ready to dive right in since I have nothing but time on my hands these days."

Fred looked across the table and saw a brief sullen moment on Keith's face and there was no doubt, his mind was also on the reason for that look.

"Do you ever talk to her? I know it's been about two years and I know how close the two of you were to getting married before she messed up. Ever hear from her again?"

He watched Keith pause without answering, no doubt thinking of how his life had been turned upside down at a point when he thought he was doing all the right things.

"No and I don't expect to. She's moved on."

"Is she still with that guy?"

Fred didn't want to say the words out loud that Keith's ex-girlfriend had cheated on him with someone they both knew.

"No, he moved on shortly after she told him that the baby she was carrying was his. She thought he would do the right thing by her, but he didn't. Last I heard, he was living with some eighteen-year-old model or something and Tamara was raising their son as a single mother. She reached out a few times after we split and we talked enough for her to explain how she could do what she did and that she felt neglected as I climbed the charts and traveled to promote my books. I was really gone a lot after I started investing in a few startup companies that took off and started bringing in the wealth. She blamed being left alone all the time while I traveled as the cause for her stepping out on me and that getting pregnant was a major slip up. You think?" Keith asserted and Fred agreed. There was no excuse.

"Did she try to reconnect with you after her son was born, even though he wasn't yours?"

"She did and I shot that down. Not that I couldn't raise a child that wasn't mine, but she walked away from me thinking he was going to marry her, though, according to her, they were not in love. What she did wasn't a one-time slipup and for that, I couldn't take her back. They'd hooked up several times and the fact that I was familiar with him bothered me. This was a guy who had been in my circle on many occasions and when he congratulated me and played pool and hung out with me, the minute I left time, he was slipping and sliding into my woman."

"And since then, you've been knee-deep in writing and building your brand. Where's the fun man? I know the women have been plentiful. You're a fairly decent looking guy," Fred quipped. "I won't even get into the rich thing and the fact that you're a good guy. Are you beating the women off with a stick?"

"Naw, dude. I'm welcoming them all with open arms, but nothing to write home about."

Fred was happy to hear that and his hopes for the

weekend were revved up by Keith's revelation that he was single.

"In other words, nothing serious?"

"Exactly. Not that they aren't worthy because all women are. You know how precious I think every single woman is and I can't wait to find what you and Renee have. Maybe I haven't thrown myself out into traffic enough to find one willing to fall in love with me after nearly running me down. That's how you met, right?" Keith joked.

Fred laughed with him.

"Best day of my life! I just knew she was going to slap me silly when I kissed her, but something took a hold of me. She was talking a mile a minute, giving me an apology for not just almost running me over, but also for giving me the finger and I couldn't take my eyes off of her. She was so damn beautiful and her lips were so perfect with that light lavender colored lip glass. I couldn't resist and let me tell you that the way she kissed me back was all I needed to sustain my life after that moment. I knew it then that she was the one and only woman for me. It happened just that fast. She was and still is feist. She practically ran me down that day and it was only a brief moment, but that was all I needed. When she showed up across the table from me, it was on like popcorn!"

"See, that's what I'm talking about. I've met and been with my share of women, but none packed a wallop of a punch like what happened to you when you met Renee. It may be because I've been so focused on work since my breakup with Tamara that I haven't given anyone a chance. Things happen right? I'm thirty-seven and still not settled down, but there is plenty of time for that. When I meet the perfect woman like you have, I will give my very limbs to prove to her that I'm ready for a life with her and only her. Anyway, enough of that talk. What are we getting into tonight? The concert isn't until tomorrow night."

"Pool. I have a buddy who owns a pool hall in the Bronx and we're heading there for a few hours tonight. Renee made me promise to not feed you while we're out because she's making her famous lasagna that you love and even if we get in late, she's going to leave it warming for us. You're only a few blocks away at the Marquis, so we're good, if that works for you."

"Sounds perfect. I love your wife's cooking. She always cooks something special when I visit you in New York. Renee is perfection, man. How did a bum like you get so lucky?" Keith joked.

Fred balled up some spare paper on the table and threw it at him. When Keith ducked, they both doubled over with laughter and stood.

"I'm glad you're here and I promise you a good time. You sure you can't stay a few extra days?"

"I don't know yet. I'm going to play it by ear. I have a flight out on Saturday afternoon and I already told you that you don't have to take me back to the airport. I also don't want to get in my sister's way of getting my condo and house together. I can always get a car back to the airport. If I decide to stay a day or two longer, I'll let you know. I love New York and there is always a reason to hang around a few extra days especially between Thanksgiving and Christmas. I want to pick up a few gifts for my sisters. Have you talked to Darren and Tyrone?"

Darren and Tyrone were their fraternity brothers from Howard who also lived in the New York area and the four of them tried to connect a few times a year.

"They're both meeting us at the pool hall once we leave here."

"So, you're not pulling late hours these days?" Keith asked.

"I love having my own business and it's very lucrative, but nothing comes before family time and connecting with my brothers when they're in town. I have an entire team who are more than capable of running things in my absence and when I need to be away, I let them do just that," he explained.

As they moved toward the conference room door to leave, he stopped when Keith stopped ahead of him.

"You mean like Monday when Renee had you tied to the bed? I can't believe you blew off an entire day of work to sex your wife up all day long. Where do people do that at?" Keith jested.

"I do and any time my wife wants my attention, I

give it to her. Nothing is more important to me than making her and the kids happy. What my woman wants is always the priority. You'll see one day. I can't wait for you to meet that woman that will make you flip off a day and spend it wrapped around her. Let me tell you about this coma my wife put me in on Monday! I mean, I'm still trying to recover days later!" Fred laughed as they left the office.

What he failed to add was that there was a possibility that Keith would know what it felt like sooner than he could ever imagine. They would all soon find out.

5

Reagan bundled up against the brisk cold while standing in line with Renee as they waited to get inside of Radio City Music Hall, the venue for the Jill Scott concert. There was no doubt, by the size of the crowd, that it was a sold-out event. Though she had been bullied into making the trip to New York, she was glad she did the moment she woke early and made her way to the train station. As she suspected, when she told her father that she needed a few days off for a trip to New York to visit Renee, he wasn't thrilled at the last-minute trip, knowing she was missing some important meetings. Unlike at other times when he guilted her into changing her mind for the sake of business, she held to the promise she made and he relented and told her to have a good time, though his face didn't match his sentiment. She was planning to do just that.

When she arrived in New York, she felt refreshed after a good night's sleep and a long nap on the train ride. She hadn't had that much sleep in a long time and if she counted good sleep, that had been even longer ago. This time off is exactly what she needed. What she didn't need was Renee showing up at her hotel as she arrived to check-in. Her sister wanted to make sure there was no laptop or other work in her weekend bag and there wasn't. She promised no work and she meant it. She did have her iPad with her, but she wouldn't check her work email. She left everything in very capable hands with the best staff she could ever have and there was no doubt that Sherry would keep everyone in line, including Buster, who was shocked to hear she was on vacation until Tuesday morning. When he started to comment about her time off during their staff meeting on Thursday afternoon, she quickly quieted him with her hand. She was just ripe for embarrassing him if he didn't say the right thing and so it was best to avoid that all the way. She knew he was eyeing her job, but as long as she was in it, she wanted him to focus on his job and work on his appreciation for women in business. He wouldn't be placed in a higher leadership role if he didn't change his mindset. She wanted to be sure no woman experienced a man trying to keep her back simply because of her gender. Even her father commented that if Buster didn't improve, he would send him packing. Time would tell.

For this weekend, she didn't want to think about any of them. Her plan was to focus on the concert and hanging with her sister for the weekend.

She went into Renee's tight hug when she grabbed her as they waited to get inside. Renee kept hugging her as if she was stocking up on hugs for a rainy day.

"I can't breathe if you keep hugging me like this!" she kidded.

"I can't help myself. I'm so happy you're here. I mean, I thought I was going to have to call in the troops if you had decided to cancel on me again."

"I told you I was coming."

"Yeah, you've said that before and yet..."

Renee didn't finish her thought and Reagan didn't need her to. She already knew what was next. She'd cancelled quite a few times, using work as the reason, but the truth was, she didn't need a live and in color view of her sister's perfect life with her perfect husband and perfect children. She loved them all more than anything in life, but that didn't mean that inside, she wasn't jealous, because she was.

Both of her sisters were living the life that dreams are made of. They had men who loved and cherished them while they still maintained careers they wanted to have with men who supported those dreams. Her last boyfriend wanted her to give up her job at the bank and follow him as he followed his own dreams, telling her that she didn't need to have a dream since he would dream big enough for them both. Too many times, he'd made her feel what she wanted didn't matter. When she forgot about plans he'd made for them, she knew it was over and though she was crushed in the beginning, she knew the end was the best for them both. Joe had found his little woman to live off of his every word. She heard the woman was now pregnant and the interesting part of the story was, she wasn't the only woman pregnant with his baby. She was glad what they had ended six months ago. The latest she heard, he was still out there philandering right in front of her face telling her that as long as he provided for her, he deserved a little fun on the side. A woman like her would take that – she never would, which made knowing that she was fine with Joe breaking up with her the best idea he'd ever had. He wasn't the first man to break up with her and he probably wouldn't be the last until there was a man who saw her as an equal and not a conquest.

"I'm here now and that's all that matters. I'm ready for a weekend of no work and all play. I hope you have a lot of fun stuff planned. I brought my favorite credit card and I'm ready for some good deals!" Reagan chimed.

"Girl, you don't need anything else filling up the closets in that big ol' house of yours. Well, maybe you do since you're going to leave this black and silver one-piece pantsuit with me when you go back home. I don't know how you keep such a perfect figure when I know how much of a foodie you are. I'm still trying to lose baby weight and Amaya is five years old!" Renee shouted.

"You can have it or I can send you your own. There is this new African-American designer that I love getting new things to wear from. She gives me a discount because she calls me one of her walking promoters. Someone even took a picture of me in a red and black body suit I bought from her and used it to show her what they wanted her to make for them. I laughed when she sent me the picture."

"You make every outfit look hot on you with your perfect features and perfectly sculpted body and let's not forget about your perfectly, glowing skin. I'm so jealous."

"I brought you some of the products I use, all from the *Fenty* line by Rhianna. I live by her products. We need to go shopping for more while I'm here. I'm running low, now that I think of it. Where is Fred? I thought he was coming?"

Reagan looked around, through the crowd waiting, thinking Fred would pop up any minute.

"He's meeting us here. Look, the line is moving. Looks like the doors are open."

Reagan's excitement was unmatched. She tried to remember the last time she'd gone to a concert. Remembering it was to see Ledisi, she couldn't imagine why she hadn't gone to more shows. Inside, she knew the real reason – she was tired of going alone.

"Yeah! Jill Scott here we come. I listened to her music on the train to get ready for tonight. I'm so excited! I can't remember the last time I saw her in concert."

"Fred and I saw her last year right at the start of the pandemic. That was our last, big outing that year," Renee said.

"I forgot the excitement that comes with knowing you will get to see your favorite artist sing right in front of you. I know a lot of people missed that for all of last year."

"You have always loved her music. I'm glad me and Fred could do this for you."

When they got inside, Reagan looked around for mementos to take back with her, including something for Sherry who made her promise to bring back at least a t-shirt. Anytime she took a trip, even for business, she tried to bring something back for her staff of eight and always doubled up on the gifts for Sherry who ran her life and the office.

"Me, too. There is a place over there to get some stuff. Let's check it out before going to our seats."

Reagan took off practically running in order to get in line before it got too long.

"For someone who was hesitant about coming, I'm out of breath keeping up with you."

She started to apologize but didn't. Since arriving earlier that afternoon, she had dragged Renee all over town with her from one store to the next before they parted to get ready for the concert.

"Hey, this was all your idea, so don't be

complaining. I'm going to have you on skates all weekend and I want massive amounts of good food. I'm already hungry just thinking about it I can't wait!" she proclaimed.

"We just had tacos before the show."

"Tacos were just a teaser. Aren't we having dinner after the show?"

"Oh, yes. A friend of Fred's owns a restaurant that has the best seafood outside of Maryland. When you eat his crab cakes, you're going to think you're in Baltimore at *Pappas* and you know how good their crab cakes are!"

"Yes, I do. I had them Wednesday – stopped to pick them up on my way home from work. I love getting the double crab cake platter with double broccoli. Takes me two days to eat it, but I don't care. It's just as good the second day. If you say this place in New York does them just as good, I trust you and I'll be trying them. Do you want a shirt or something else? I'm next and you know they want you to know what you want when it's your time. I swear, New Yorkers have no patience!"

Reagan looked at her choices and saw three shirts she wanted and two sweatshirts. She didn't get the chance to dress down often, but when she did, she would be sporting her Jill Scott gear.

"No, I'm good. Shop 'til you drop, sis! I'm going to hit the restroom before we go in. Should I wait for you?" Renee asked.

Reagan was already planning on doing that. If she was going to be in New York for four days, she was going to make the best of the trip. There was no telling when she'd be able to take time off like this again; probably never, if their father had any say.

"No, you go ahead; I'm good. What door should I meet you at since you have the tickets?" Reagan asked as she ignored the clerk behind the counter who annoyingly kept screaming the word, 'next' at her.

"End of the aisle here at the first set of double doors and we'll go in together."

"Okay."

Turning back around, Reagan was about to tell the woman what she wanted when the woman looked beyond her and asked the man to her left if she could help him. From the silly look on the woman's face, she knew the man must be fine, especially when the woman fluffed up her long blond wig and licked her lips. Turning to see who the clerk was looking at, she came face-to-face with a strikingly hunk of deliciousness who was smiling, from ear to ear. Was he flirting back with the woman or just a happy guy? Either way, his smile was electric and she couldn't look away. She quickly took in everything about him.

Knowing that she herself loved nice, designer clothing, she noted his pristine black bomber leather jacket which was opened to show a black buttoned-down shirt and when she looked down, the rest of him took her breath away. She had a thing for men with that ever-present bow to his legs and covering them were the sexiest pair of blue denim jeans. Goodness, she loved a man who could wear a nice pair of jeans. When she looked down, they were covering what looked like a pair of black Dr. Martens boots, characterized by their yellow stitching and expensive looking high tops. She knew attire and this guy was wearing it well. When her eyes traveled back up his body to his face, she found that she'd been caught admiring and staring. When she should have looked away, she didn't. His face was too handsome to just quickly glance at him. The perfect goatee, neatly trimmed to his close-cut haircut, with not only waves, but tiny, perfect curls and then eyes, a light brown shade had her feeling like a moth being pulled into a hot flame and not caring that she was about to get burned. Damn!

"I'm sorry? Were you speaking to me?" he asked.

Reagan was suddenly thrust back into the reality of where she was and the fact that the word may not have been only in her head, but accidentally spoken out loud.

"Oh, I'm sorry. I think you're next. She's trying to get your attention," she stuttered out.

Saving herself from embarrassment, she pointed to the clerk and watched as his head turned toward her. Then the most amazing thing happened; he leaned down toward her. The natural reaction would have been to move away thinking he was inserting himself in front of her, but she stood still as desire like nothing she'd ever known surfaced with the need to have him closer.

"Shame. I was hoping you had said something to me in order to start a conversation; any kind of conversation," he said.

As his husky voice cascaded over her, she felt his words tingle every part of her; even her toes jumped. The face and the voice were familiar, but with the lighting not being the best, she couldn't place why. All she knew was that she wasn't too far out of the game to know when a man was flirting with her and an intoxicating zing surged through her at the possibility.

"Miss? Are you going to order anything or should I give you a camera and you can just take a picture of him?" the clerk asked in a nasty tone that drew Reagan's attention her way with a sneer of unappreciation.

"Don't hate the player or the game," she responded in kind.

"Haha," the man said behind her and Reagan smiled harder.

"I'll take the first three t-shirts on the front row, all in a large and both of the sweatshirts in extra-large," she said.

"Great choices. Now I know what to get for my sisters," he said behind her.

Reagan wanted to engage him, but knew that doing so would only irk the clerk even more since the line was getting longer and the show would be starting soon. Paying for her order, she turned around to finally respond to him and perhaps give him her name when she came face to face with a man who appeared to be in his sixties, handsome, but not the tall sexy man who had been standing there. To show that she needed to back off, the woman with him grabbed him tight as if to make sure there was no doubt of who he belonged to. Smiling politely, she looked around and saw the same man with whom she wanted to be engaging with being waited on by someone else. The crowd thickened and he was soon out of sight.

Feeling a tug on her arm, she turned and saw Renee pulling on her.

"Come on. Fred sent me a text that he's already at our seats. Are you ready?" she asked.

Exhaling her frustration of not getting the chance to say a few words to the handsome stranger, she walked off as Renee pulled her along.

"I have the worse timing," she said.

"What?" Renee asked.

"Oh, nothing."

Reagan looked back again and didn't see him at all. As they entered the doors and headed toward the front, she was happy to see that they were on the end of the third row from the stage, dead center; perfect seats. When Fred turned and saw them, he stood and hugged her and kissed Renee like he was just coming home from a war.

"More later?" Renee asked and Reagan faked like she was gagging.

"Ugh, get a room, brother-in-law!" Reagan said and hugged him tight.

"Oh, I plan to do that and that room had better be sound proof," he laughed. "We're here in the first four seats," he said.

Reagan started to move into the row and then stopped.

"Four?" she asked and knew something was up the minute her sister looked at her husband with enough guilt to send a defendant to jail for life. When Renee began to stutter, she knew.

"Oh, yeah, a friend of Fred's is joining us for the show. Did I forget to tell you?"

Leaning back and looking them both over, Reagan pointed between the two of them as she realized what was up. As she pointed, their innocent faces didn't work on her.

"Tell me you didn't? Never mind, I can see it on your faces. You set me up, didn't you? You both set me up. Who's coming and why would you do that?" she exclaimed loudly, trying to talk over the roar of the everyone entering and trying to find their seats.

"I am."

Reagan didn't move. She didn't have the strength to turn around. Her legs felt like jelly and she was glad there was a seat on her left that kept her from melting to the floor as she grabbed the back of it and held tightly to the wood to steady herself. She knew that voice. She'd heard it in the lobby; a voice she'd never forget. Just like before, the sound of it melted her insides.

Turning slowly, she came eye to eye with her lobby crush.

"Wha...what?" she stammered out.

"Reagan, this is Keith Jackson, a friend of Fred's. Keith, this is my sister Reagan who also just happens to live near Baltimore where you just moved to. Reagan, Keith is joining us for the concert tonight. Come on into the aisle so we can all sit down. Fred is going to sit here on the end, then me and Keith you can sit next to me and then Reagan. I think I'm going to need a buffer between me and my sister."

Reagan threw fire with her eyes. She was mad and happy at the same time, but first, she wanted to be angry that her sister would set her up. That anger quickly turned to happiness that her sister had set her up.

Moving to her seat, she sat down as Keith took the seat to her left.

"Nice to see you again. The first time was so brief," Keith said.

When he held out his hand for her to shake, Reagan took it and felt a spark as if she'd been standing on carpet. When normal people would have shaken hands and then let go, she held on as long as he gripped her hand. They locked eyes and everyone else in the place fell away, leaving just the two of them. Never in her lifetime had she ever had such an impactful introduction to anyone; especially a man; a hot, sexy, gorgeous, *fine as hell* kind of man.

"Yes, from the lobby. Imagine that. What a coincidence, huh?" she asked as they sat and she looked beyond him, rolling her eyes at Renee. She'd deal with her intrusion later.

"I don't believe in coincidences. Do you know what I believe in?" he leaned over and asked her.

She felt his breath on her ear, where it tickled her senseless. The feeling was electrifying.

Ignoring Renee who was smiling from ear to ear, she looked up again into eyes that were like ocean waves inviting her in. She had to clear her throat to speak, finding her tongue again.

"No – what?"

When Keith leaned closer, almost close enough to kiss her on the lips, she held her breath and waited for his next word or even a hot kiss. She would accept either.

"Fate."

6

To say that he thought his day was starting out as a great one after getting a call from his agent that Jamie Foxx was on board to play the lead character in his movie trilogy, would be an understatement of what a great day was. Keith didn't have time to pull his best friends' card for setting him up on, what he now believed was a blind date, because where he would have scolded him for doing so, he wanted to shake his hand and appreciate that he was the man sitting next to the most beautiful woman in the entire world. That was his first thought when he saw her standing in line in the lobby, but now being this close to her again, what he thought was a chance encounter was now the meeting of a lifetime. He would thank Fred later, maybe even buy him an island or some other extravagant gift. The woman next to him stirred every bone in his body; every one of them.

As soon as he walked up and saw her, he couldn't take his eyes off of her and it was clear that she felt the same way. He wasn't sure that she knew she'd been caught eyeing him from head to toe and he was hoping against all hope that she liked what she saw because he sure did.

Keith wasn't shy about the fact that the first thing that caught his attention was her behind in what looked like a black jumpsuit with silver accents. No man could miss her sexy, curvy body and he was no exception. He'd never seen a backside, one so perfect on a woman, so expertly round, expertly designed. The only thing he knew for sure was that the outfit was made for what he saw; faultlessness. When she turned his way, all he saw was beauty and the way she was looking at him with appreciation, mirrored his appreciation for a woman's beauty, especially the one who stood before him.

He loved her thick, long, curly hair. He saw and felt her smile when he whispered to her and though they weren't touching, that meeting was electric for him, a new experience at first encountering a woman. He had been hoping for more of a chance to talk with her until one of the clerks urged him forward to make his purchase and he didn't want to hold everyone up. He looked up afterward and no longer saw her as his hopes of at least getting her number had dashed away. As fate would have it, he would get a second chance and not being a person to chance fate, he was going to make the most of the night. After only mere seconds, he knew he wasn't leaving New York without a way to connect with her beyond the concert and she lived in the Baltimore area where he'd just moved to. He smiled at the planets that were aligned in his favor.

Since they only had a chance to exchange pleasantries before the concert started, he had hoped for an intermission or some other chance to talk more. He had to get to know her.

In any other setting with Jill Scott on stage, he wouldn't be able to take his eyes off of the songstress, having been a fan for years, but tonight, every chance he could, he looked at Reagan and took in more of her. When she stood to dance to the music, he stood with her and when they acted like they were dancing together and laughing while getting the most from the concert, he went with the comfortable flow of connecting with her that way. He was picturing them in a nightclub, dancing and grooving without a care in the world. After almost an hour, Jill Scott took a break for a quick change of attire and he took that chance to engage Reagan as the band played through her absence.

"I see you're enjoying yourself," he said, leaning in her direction.

"I am having the time of my life. Are you?" she asked.

Keith wanted to express how tonight would go down in the record books as one of the best of his life, but he didn't want to get that deep and scare her off. If he was truly lucky, he would have time to do that.

"I am loving it and I'm glad you're my seat-mate. I've been wanting to see her in concert for a while now. I'm glad Fred was able to get these good seats."

"How do you know Fred?" she asked him.

"We are friends and fraternity brothers from Howard. I used to live on the west coast and therefore, didn't get to see him often, but now I live on this coast and he and I are going into business together," he explained.

"Reagan, I'm running to the ladies room. You want to go?" Renee leaned over and asked.

Reagan waved her off while keeping her eyes on Keith.

"No, I'm good. Fred can walk you, right Fred?" she asked politely and Keith laughed at their response to her. Both got up and left immediately.

"Wow, you sure know how to clear a room!" he chimed.

When Reagan laughed heartily, he laughed with her and enjoyed her jovial response.

"I know my sister. She was going to ask me a million questions about whether or not I liked you and if I was going to be mad at her forever for setting me up, which is what this is. You know that, right?"

"I did the moment I saw you here with them. I swear I didn't know about this ahead of time," he said.

"I didn't either."

"I'm not mad though," he added and locked on her gaze.

"Neither am I. Wait, I know you. You're Keith Jackson, the author. You're *that* Keith Jackson? Oh, my goodness, I have your last three books and I love them. I had no idea you knew Fred."

"Only the last three books?" Keith joked.

"I don't get a lot of time to read, but I heard about the first one and after I read it in a day, I had to get the other two. I love the entire series. I was planning on getting your back reads. Work gets in the way of fun stuff like book shopping. It was definitely on my to-do list to get more of your books and I'm not just saying that because you're sitting here next to me."

"I'm glad you enjoyed them and when you get a few of the later books, you will see a dedication to Fred and your sister. I thanked him for a lifetime of friendship and your sister helped me out after my books really took off. I didn't know what to do with the influx of income and Renee fixed my life. Are you in finance too? I know she's not now, but she was when I needed her."

"Yes, I work in the banking industry where she used to work."

"You work with your father, Ernest?" he asked.

Keith was checking in on fate and really wondered what was happening. He'd just met the most unforgettable woman and they shared a connection beyond wanting to know more about each other.

"You know my father?" she asked him.

Keith could not believe the perfect woman was

this close and he'd never met her before now. He would slam Fred later for waiting this long to introduce him to Reagan. What was his best friend waiting for? Perhaps, she had been involved with someone before now. Maybe she still was. He didn't know and he didn't care. He was officially throwing his hat in the ring for her attention.

"Your sister introduced me to your father years ago. They worked together on my investment portfolio. He introduced me to the best funds management specialist and it was the best partnership of my life, until this moment. Wow, what a small world. I'm surprised our worlds haven't met before now. I'll have to ask Fred about that later."

"Ask Fred what?"

"Why he hasn't introduced me to you before now. Were you married? Engaged? Involved in a serious relationship? Are you any of those now?" he inquired.

Keith didn't care that his many questions made him seem exposed – he needed to know if he was staring at his chance to see if the best decision he ever made in life was to come to New York at this time in his life after making countless number of trips to the region for business. He'd known Fred for years and not once did he mention that Renee had a single sister. He knew she had sisters and assumed they were all married.

"None of the above and if my sister hadn't laid guilt on me about cancelling on her for other trips to get together, this meeting may not have happened either."

"A plus for me. Like I said, it's not a coincidence or happenstance, it's pure fate. I was meant to meet you or my radar is off because from the second I saw you in line, I wanted to meet you; I had to meet you and then you were gone. Low and behold, here you are again, just as beautiful as you were when I spotted you in the lobby and you're sitting in the seat next to me; another plus for me."

He was saying too much too fast. He was going to scare her away. Looking at Reagan's emotionless face, he felt like he was being too aggressive and not all women liked that.

"I have to admit that I was checking you out too. I think I was quite obvious."

"You were, but a gentleman never calls that to attention in case the woman wanted to do it without feeling uncomfortable. How did I do?" he smiled and turned his head to give her a look at him from every angle.

"Whew."

Before he could respond to her one word and ask what it meant, they were rejoined by Renee and Fred.

"Enjoying the show?" Renee asked them.

"Yes," Keith and Reagan said in unison.

"Told you," Fred said to Renee and they all looked to him for an explanation, but none came.

Keith didn't need it. All he needed was time to get

to know the woman next to him and time to let her get to know him. He wondered quietly, how early he could call and change his flight back to Baltimore. He didn't know how long she would be in town, but if she was going to be around for a few days, he was hoping to join her in whatever she would like to do.

"Are you joining us for dinner after the show?" Reagan asked.

"I wouldn't miss it."

"You're living in Baltimore now I think I heard Renee say?"

"Yes, and you as well? What part are you in? I know the bank is in downtown Baltimore. I've been there a few times to meet with your father."

"I live in one of the surrounding counties, in Bel Air, Maryland which is in Harford County. I used to live in a downtown condo, but I wanted a backyard and a pool. What part of Baltimore did you move to?"

"I bought a condo in the Ritz Carlton in downtown Baltimore, Federal Hill."

"Wow, those are amazing. I looked at them at one time, but the desire to have a house overtook me, but those were a close second after my condo became too small for me and I wanted more space."

"I wanted one because of the view of the inner harbor, which is magnificent. I had a house when I lived in California and I bought one in Maryland as well, but I also wanted to live on the water and that condo was in the middle of everything. There's a lot to do in Baltimore and I look forward to taking it all in."

"I love California, especially Santa Monica Pier."

"I'm not far from there in Malibu overlooking the ocean. I technically still have it, but I don't plan on being in it too often with all of the work I'll have on this coast. I wanted to keep it for when I do travel that way. I love the view. It's second in beauty only to your beauty and I don't mean that as a line – it's what I thought in the second after we saw each other in the lobby," he admitted and waited to see if he'd said too much. When she blushed and smiled over at him, he exhaled.

"Thank you."

"My pleasure. What do you do at the bank?" he asked, taking the heaviness out of their conversation. He was planning on a time for more later.

Keith had a million questions and his mind raced through all of them. He wanted to be sure she gathered that he was more than casually interested in her because he was. It was fate that they met and that they were going to be living close by. As Jill came back out on the stage and joined her band, the concert restarted, but neither of them cared as they continued to talk. They moved closer together to hear each other. When Jill Scott came out singing, *He Loves Me (Lyzel in E Flat)*, nothing could be more perfect for the moment he was sharing with Reagan. He would never forget the song and it was now his all-time favorite song, ever.

"I'm a senior vice president over operations and expansion."

"That's fascinating. Congratulations! I know you worked hard for that level of achievement. I admire you," he said.

The look on her face was one of mystery. Did he insult her? He thought back over his words and hoped that they were complimentary.

"Thank you. I don't often get that response. Thank you," she said.

He was stumped. Who wouldn't compliment such an achievement?

"You don't? What do you usually get?"

"People who tell me I got it because my father owns the bank. I especially get that from men."

"Well, they're pitiful and probably jealous. No gets a position like that without someone seeing their potential and hard work and it's disrespectful to think anyone can't work for what they have. Do you enjoy what you do?"

"It's a lot and has taken over my life. My sister invited me here for the weekend because she said I don't live enough for today or any day, if you let her tell it."

"Do you feel that way?"

"Honestly? Until this very moment, I thought I was living."

Keith fell hard, unashamedly. Who does this? He sure never has, but something was telling him that

Reagan wasn't just any woman.

"And now?"

"Something is telling me that I've been missing out on the good parts of life. This should be an interesting couple of days."

"Am I being too forward if I say that I'd like to take you out to dinner or anything while we're both in New York? I'd love a chance to let you know more about me."

"How long are you here for?" she asked him.

Keith smiled at her and spoke directly into her hear.

"As long as it takes."

7

At the end of the show, Reagan couldn't stop clapping. Not only was the concert great, but the music and the ambience along with the man seated next to her made for an unbelievable night. She was over the moon and high from excitement, hating that the show was coming to an end along with her closeness with Keith. Within two hours of meeting, the man had broken through every barrier she had up when it came to men. For some reason, she felt like she had to remain on the defense with them, but Keith dispelled that notion by being open and attentive. Most of all, if there was any reason that she was doubtful of his interest in her, it was all her because no man could be more obvious and to her own delight, she was just as interested in him.

As Jill Scott left the stage and the lights went up in the theater, everyone stood to leave except for her and Keith; they remained seated. It was unspoken, but neither wanted to leave. When she looked up, Renee was looking at her with a stupid grin on her face.

"Are we interrupting?" Renee asked.

"Yes, you are, but it's okay," Reagan said and stood.

"Dinner?" Keith asked Fred and then looked to her and Renee, questionably.

He looked to be thinking the same thoughts as her, that the night was already turning out to be too short. She was about to speak up when Renee spoke first.

"Ugh, Fred and I are really exhausted. We thought we would be hungry, but we're not. We're going to head home and take advantage of our child-free evening, but the reservation is still in his name and we want the two of you to go and enjoy dinner on us. Whatever you want is already paid for. Or, should we join you anyway?"

Reagan knew the sign of what Renee was fishing for. She wanted to know if she liked Keith enough to have dinner with him alone or if she needed company as a filter for a match not meant to be.

"Go home and do what the two of you do when you don't have your kids for the night and when you feel the need to tell me about it later, don't. I'm fine having dinner with Keith if he's up for it being just the two of us."

When she turned to him, he turned to Fred and Renee.

"I hope the two of you have a good night and I'll

be sure to get Reagan back to you in one piece and at a semi-decent hour since it's already ten. Thanks for the ticket to the show. I can't tell you how incredible this night is turning out to be," he said.

"I'm not staying with them and I'm way beyond a curfew. I'm a few blocks away at the Marquis," she interrupted to explain. She didn't know why she felt the need to give more information than was needed, but she did it anyway.

"I'm staying there too," Keith added.

When Fred cleared his throat, drawing their attention, she knew he did so to avoid being questioned about all of the coincidences happening in one night.

"Well, I guess that's it then. Bro, you'll holler before you leave tomorrow? I'll text you the address to the restaurant and when you get there, give them my name," Fred said.

"Uh, yeah, I'll be in touch. I may hang around for an extra day or two or three. I'll let you know."

Reagan smiled inwardly and tried with everything in her to contain her joy. Sounds to her like Keith wasn't going to be leaving New York as she assumed he would and she was ecstatic.

"Sis, we're supposed to go shopping tomorrow around noon. Call me and I'll walk over to your hotel if that works?" Renee asked.

"Yeah, shopping sounds good. I'll see you tomorrow."

Reagan hugged and kissed them before they turned and walked away leaving her standing in a nearly empty theater with Keith. Now that they were alone, she didn't know what to say or do. She'd been on quite a few dates over the years and a few ended with a man, after getting to know her, telling her that he was a little intimidated by her and what she'd achieved in life or that she didn't appear to have time for a man in her life. What would Keith think? Still, she was up for the challenge and looked forward to having dinner with him.

"I guess that's that. You're sure you're okay having dinner with me? I'm really up for that as long as you're comfortable with me," he said.

"If my brother-in-law trusts you, I'm more than up for it. I know them and how overprotective they are of me. They easily left me here with you without question."

Keith's cell phone pinged.

"Shall we go? Fred just sent me the address to the restaurant and said it's less than a ten-minute walk. Those boots you have on are sexy as hell, but are they comfortable for walking? I can always call us a car."

"Oh, they are high, but very comfortable. The soles are very soft. I can walk. It's not too cold out, so I'm good."

When she stepped out of the row behind him, she smiled to herself when he searched for her hand and placed it in the crook of his arm. She held on tight and walked with him toward the exit. She gave his arm a slight squeezed and rejoiced at the toned muscle she felt there. Sexy and muscles? She was in heaven!

Reaching the front door, she watched Keith walk with a purpose, his strides at a pace that made keeping up with him easy. He was making sure he didn't walk faster than the legs of her five-foot, nine-inch height in heels could carry her. Keith had to be over six-feet tall, since he towered over her, even in her heels. She loved tall men; another check on her list for how much she liked him.

"Have you been to the restaurant before?" she asked as they walked.

"No."

"Oh, you seem to already know where you're going."

"I love New York and I've been here a lot and when Fred sent me the address, I knew exactly where it was."

"You said you have something you're working on with Fred? Is that here in New York?" she asked.

"No, it's actually happening in Maryland. Fred and I are building a production studio and we're going to soon begin filming the first movie of a trilogy based on my last three novels, the ones you have. It's going to be huge. There's an announcement coming out in early March about our project. Studios have been trying to buy the rights from me to make the movies, but I held out. Since I'm not starving for money, not that more wouldn't be great, Fred and I got with some silent partners we trust and decided to do this on our own. We have already hired some great writers to help turn the books into movie manuscripts. The finances are in place and we have the location in mind that we've bought from the city and now, we wait until all the rest of the ducks are in a row."

"Is that why you moved to Maryland?"

"It is and now more than any other time since I've been making the decision about moving, I'm glad I did. If by the end of the night, you don't think I'm some kind of Shrek, you know, an ogre unworthy of your time, I hope that I can take you out when we're back in Maryland. Again, that's if you don't give me the brush off after dinner. If I'm messing up before we get back to the hotel, promise you'll tell me and give me a chance to redeem myself."

Reagan looked up at him, not sure if he was serious or joking, but she laughed anyway.

"You are all green lights," she responded confidently and honestly.

For now, she held back on any more questions. She wanted to take in the fact that she was walking the streets of New York City holding on to the finest man she'd ever seen and one who she knew would appreciate her hardworking lifestyle because he was her mirror when it came to work ethic. She hummed along to the Christmas music she heard in the air. New York was so alive even at this hour of night.

When she heard Keith humming along with her, she was imagining this is what it felt like when a couple focused on enjoyment and nothing else and she liked it, as much as she liked Keith.

She knew who he was as far as his writing and she looked forward to learning more directly from him on more of a personal level before she did what anyone else would do; checked him out on the internet.

She was already taking in everything about him. The way he took her hand and placed it in his arm and held on just tight enough to make sure she felt safe and secure had her smiling like a school girl. She was on a date; she was in New York and she was on a date and that excited her. Just the idea of it made her happier than she's been in a long time. Work had become her escape from a doldrum life of not having much else going on. Sure, she had lots of friends and could hang out with them anytime she wanted, but she chose not to. She was tired of fielding questions about her lack of a personal life.

There were men who approached her all the time, but for some reason, she shot them down without even giving them a chance. Her immediate response was always that she wasn't interested either by her words or by her actions. Most found her standoffish and didn't want to approach her and those that did, never received a vibe that she was remotely interested and so they left her alone.

Her last date had been in early November. That

had been Napoleon – a guy with a strange name for this day and time, but clearly, his parents had high hopes. She'd gone out and had a great time with him, more than once. Then one night he brought up the subject of her getting him a sit-down meeting with her father about a business idea he had and wanted her to back him because if she did, her father may be more apt to his idea of a business partnership. She blocked his number and found out that the day she'd met him wasn't by chance. He was friends with one of the security guards at the bank office building who told Napoleon who she was. That happened more than a few times and she was already over it happening again.

Before him, she'd met Terrence back in September. He was someone who was still trying to find himself. He was fine and knew it, but was also on the prowl for a woman who was doing big things so that he could stop working his regular nine to five job and pursue his dream as a boxer. He figured, if he could meet a woman who could hold him down while he followed his dreams, she was a keeper. What she heard was a brother looking for a sponsor. She met that type a lot as well. She still remembered the first time she invited him to her house, by the end of the night, he was a little too comfortable in her spot and he mentioned how he could see himself being in her house with her all the time. She was annoyed.

There were times when wished she could meet

someone who really wanted her for her and not for what she had or what she could do for them. Who was Keith, she wondered? She was in New York and clearly, she had been set up to meet him by her sister and one thing was certain, Renee did not play when it came to her sisters. If anyone knew her struggles with dating, it was her. She had shared on more than one occasion that she would love to have a good man in her life and was open to exploring a serious relationship, but those kinds of relationships didn't seem to come for her. Instead, she started settling for letting work be the only sustaining relationship in her life. Until this trip to New York, she was okay with that. Her immediate attraction to Keith showed her that she hadn't give up on the prospect of much more.

When she locked in on him at the concert venue, she had no idea they would now be on their way to dinner together. To her, life was funny that way. When she called for a car to take her to the train station to get to New York, she started to change her mind and have the driver take her to the office instead. What a loss that would have been for her. She was in New York for a reason and she was ready to embrace the good and if need be, the bad. She silently hoped for all good and no bad. It was time.

"We're here," Keith said.

"This place looks nice," she said as he opened the door and walked in behind her.

"Good evening," the hostess said.

"Hello and good evening. We have a reservation under the name of Frederick Boston. It may say four, but there are only two of us tonight," he said.

"Oh, yes, Mr. Jackson. Mr. Boston called and said to expect you and Ms. Kelly. If you will follow me, I have the perfect table for you."

Reagan looked around as they walked. To say the place was high-end would be an understatement. It was beautiful and rich looking. She loved fine dining, often not able to enjoy it unless she was out with a group of friends or at a business dinner. That non-dating thing stood out in her life like a sore thumb. There were a lot of things she'd like to do if she was in a relationship; similar to nights like tonight.

Removing her coat with Keith's help, she slid inside of the booth across from him as he removed his own coat and placed them both on the end of his seat before sitting down.

Was her mouth hanging open? She wasn't sure because all she could do was take in the magnitude of how chiseled he appeared to be. He had a confidence about the way he moved, even to sit down, that had her shuddering in her seat. Now, this is a man, she thought. She saw the platinum watch on one wrist and the thick platinum link bracelet on the other. He loved nice things and there was nothing wrong with that. She was the same; another check on her list.

"Nice place," he said to her as she picked up the menu the hostess left for her.

"Yes, it is. I wouldn't expect anything else from Fred. He and my sister come here a lot. She mentioned that to me one time. He takes her to the best places and they're always finding new places to go to on their date nights. I love their love."

Reagan could shoot herself. Why did she have to bring up anything about love? She'd just met Keith and already inserting the "L" word into the conversation. Strike one against her.

"I always tell them that they have the perfect love," Keith said.

She then knew the word wasn't taboo; he'd just said it too.

"Do you know how they met?" she asked.

Reagan remembered Renee calling her the night that Fred had kissed her in an elevator. That same night, Renee also told her that she'd just met her future husband and then, it was so. Did love really happen that easily? It had to be true because it happened that way for both of her sisters.

"I do and told Fred that one day, I'm going to help him write a book about it," Keith joked.

"It was crazy, like something out of a romance novel. They fell in love in an elevator."

"Actually, he told me he fell in love the minute she gave him the finger right after she almost hit him. He loved her spunk and then when he saw her in action at the meeting, he said he was already picking out her engagement ring in his head. I remember Fred during our time on campus at Howard and he never had that kind of a reaction to any woman; never. We lost contact for a time after college when I moved to the west coast when I was chasing dreams and all. When we reconnected, he had been married to Renee about a year and he walked me through their entire romance. You're right; it's definitely something out of a romance novel. They are living an entire life of happily ever after and it couldn't have happened to two better people, in my opinion. What about you? Have you ever been in love?"

Reagan didn't want to lie, but was it good conversation to focus on past relationships? He asked her, so she should answer.

"I thought I was, but he had other ideas. That was years ago when I first graduated from college. He dumped me. I guess I wasn't good girlfriend material, but I dodged a bullet. That's all I'll say about that."

There she goes, giving too much information again.

"His loss. Like you, I've had my share of bad relationships and I simply chalk them up to not being the right person for me."

Reagan thought about those words from him as they placed their orders. She ordered the steak and crab cake entrée while Keith ordered the fish of the day and crab cake. They ordered vegetables to share.

"Do you believe in there being a right person?" she asked. Since they were talking relationships, she wanted to hear his innermost thoughts on the subject.

"I believe in there being a right person coming along at the right moment and when that happens, it makes for the kind of happiness that Renee and Fred have along with so many other couples who make it work every day. Who wouldn't want to find the right person? I thought I had at one point in my life, but forces beyond my control opened my eyes to my reality and it wasn't the kind of happiness I thought I was living. That passed and I moved on. Since then, I've been engrossed in my life as an author and soon a movie writer and executive producer. I've carved out a nice niche in life for myself, but I see that there is something, someone missing. I've never slowed down long enough over the past few years in order to find what I don't have."

Reagan was hearing Keith's passion from his heart and she understood. He was saying a lot of what she'd been feeling over the years, but how could she turn her back on her father and what he was trying to prepare her for? She was left as the one to help fulfill his dreams of having an heir to leave the family business to. That was her life and until she found a way to balance things better, she had to keep her focus on that. What was unexpected sat right in front of her. He was suave and charming; the kind of man a woman would love to call her own.

"How do you like Baltimore so far?" she asked, changing the subject.

"I love it. I haven't spent a lot of time there yet with the recent move, but I look forward to checking it out. I know the city gets a lot of bad press, but there are a lot of hardworking people in Baltimore who love their city and now it's my city. I will do my part to lend myself to where I can be of service. I'm hoping to bring lots of job to the area with the new studio and with the shooting of the three movies. A lot of the scenes will take place in D.C. and Virginia as well as Maryland and I'm already putting in a request to use as many people from the community for walk-on roles as possible. We have a while before any of that happens. For now, I need to work on unpacking and getting settled in. One of my sisters, Erika, is at my place now working on ideas for designing the place and overseeing the unpacking. It needs a lot of work and there is a ton of space. My sister has her work cut out for her, but she's ready for it. She's using that degree she has in interior design. She's very successful at it in Los Angeles."

"How many siblings do you have?"

"Just the two sisters, Erika and Erin. I'm the oldest and Erika is the older of the two girls. Erin is still in college in Florida where my parents live. She'll be graduating in another year. She's just happy to be on campus after doing her classes online during the pandemic. Glad that's over with and life is getting back to some level of normalcy, especially for her. I wanted her to have the campus life experience. She's planning to visit me over Spring break, so I'm rushing Erika to have my sister's room at my condo ready before then. They are on the phone everyday looking at samples and picking out bedroom and office furniture. Two of the rooms on the lower level are hers and besides the bedroom, she wanted an office setup. I think she believes she'll be spending more time with me than I have planned, but it's fine. She likes to bombard my life. I don't mind having her around as long as she focuses on school while also having fun. She can't get these younger years back and I don't want her to miss anything. The pandemic has us all appreciating life and enjoyment better."

"Yes, that was a hard time, but thankfully the world is resetting and picking itself back up."

"Agreed. What are your plans for being here in New York, for how long? You said you spend all of your time working and that this is a much-needed break for you. What are your plans?" he asked again.

Reagan hadn't thought far beyond shopping and hanging out with Renee and her family and now, she was hoping that she would be able to add Keith into some of her plans. She may not be looking at something that could be described as long-term or forever like what her sister has, but she was open for a fun weekend and was willing to let the term, fun, describe itself.

"Four days; until Monday evening. Renee has stuff planned to keep me busy and my mind off of work."

"When was your last vacation?"

Reagan was ashamed to say that she couldn't remember. When she looked over at him without answering, he got the message that it was too long ago to even matter. She was finally able to measure the level of obsession she had over work just from him asking about vacation and she hated that she couldn't remember her last fun getaway out of town that wasn't about work.

"I see it on your face and yes, it was that long ago for me. So long ago that I can't even remember," she admitted.

"You should change that. I've learned from my own mistakes of being too wrapped up in my work that life will pass you by if you let it. The question is, are you going to be an active participant or a person on the sidelines watching everyone else live the kind of life you'd like to have? I can't tell you how I would go from writing one book after another and I have manuscripts stockpiled. I was completely focused on work and some businesses where I'm an investor; too focused on that and I needed to do better. That's my plan for my new life on the east coast."

She liked that. Keith was passing out wisdom and making her see that her focus was off, but she didn't know how to reset it. This weekend, she didn't want to worry about it. If she could have four days of fun before returning to her life, she was chasing that fun down and wrangling it into submission.

"I'm trying to find my lane now. All I can promise myself is this weekend. Real life happens for me again on Tuesday morning," she admitted.

Their food was arriving and as the waiter placed their plates in front of them, she stared at the crab cake and hoped it tasted as good and friendly as it looked.

"Before we eat, I want to ask you a question and then let's shift to lighter subjects. Fair?" Keith asked.

"Let's do it."

"Okay, here it is. You seem like an extremely busy woman, focused on her career and I respect that. I don't want you to think I'm looking down on you or your priorities because as I've said, I admire it. I do want to make you an offer. I'm going to hang around until Monday and for the next three days, I want to steal all of your time. I know your sister may be angry that I'm asking to do that, but I am, and you and me meeting was her game plan, so I think she'll be okay with it. You said you don't have a lot of fun, but this weekend, I want to show you how to have an immeasurable amount of fun. I want to also put work aside for the next couple of days and find every great thing about New York and dive right in. I don't take enough time away from work and it sounds like you don't either. Now is our opportunity to push work to the back burner together. I want to make this weekend unforgettable, just in case you don't get the chance to have another free moment for a long time. You'll be able to look back and say that for this weekend, you truly had the time of your life. You think of some things you want to do and I'll do the same. We'll look at our lists and just go for it. What do you say?"

Keith wasn't offering her anything beyond the weekend and that was probably because she had already relayed to him that her career was first and he didn't want to try and steer her away from what she wanted in life. He wanted to offer her the here and now and that was all she could focus on.

She looked over at him, smiled with the biggest smile she could pull out of herself.

"Deal!"

8

Renee tossed uncomfortably from one side to the other in the king-sized bed next to Fred who was sound asleep. With no movement from the other side of the bed, she sufficed that she was the only one worried about whether or not Reagan was having a good time with Keith. She had expected a call or at least a text by now since it was well after midnight. She and Fred trusted Keith and weren't worried about him keeping Reagan safe. What she was feeling was more along the lines of being nosey than it was worry. Keith was an amazing man and Reagan was a dynamic woman and she the two of them together would be the perfect combination. How could it not be when she had a hand in them meeting?

Turning over again, she kicked the covers off of her body in frustration that her mind couldn't rest. The thin, silk nightie felt tight and constraint and even the room felt like it was closing in on her. It was all in her mind, but she couldn't help the way frustration played out with her.

She reached for her cell phone on the night stand, checking it to be sure the volume was turned all the way up. Seeing that it was, she placed it back and again, moved about anxiously, reaching for it again and putting it back. She was going to drive herself crazy. Her mind screamed for Reagan to call and let her in on how their time together was going.

"Stop it and go to sleep. Reagan is fine. You know Keith isn't going to allow anything to happen to her," Fred muttered in a sleepy, lazy voice, barely audible since his face was buried in his pillow.

She looked over at him and wondered how he could be so calm.

"Did I wake you?" she asked, already knowing the answer.

Fred shifted and even in the dark, she could see that he had turned over to face her.

"Really? You think I want to be up at this hour and not be making love to my wife? If you're going to keep me up, you need to get naked or something!" he yelled.

Renee swatted at him and then the room was illuminated with light from the lamp on his side of the bed.

"You have been all over me since we came home after the concert. Now that I think about it, I didn't even get dinner. How can you think about more sex right now? Oh, maybe that's what Reagan and Keith are doing. Wouldn't that be great? I keep telling her that she needs to schedule in something really good and nasty to get the stick out of her butt. She works too damn hard and I blame my father."

"Baby, you're a broken record. Reagan is a big girl and can think for herself. Whatever choices she makes, she makes them because she wants to and not because your father has her in front of a firing squad."

"Whatever you say. Go back to sleep. I'm sorry I woke you up."

"Oh, so a brother can't get any more loving tonight, but we can talk about your sister's love life? Look, I'm up now and so are other parts of me. Either go back to sleep or get that nightie off and jump on me. I'm too tired to put in any more work tonight. Okay, I'm lying – that's not true. I just want you to have your way with me," he kidded.

"Yeah, right. I've woken up plenty of nights to find you poking me after claims of being tired. Where do you think she is? It's after midnight. Can you call the restaurant and see if they are still there? You can do that without Reagan knowing we're spying on them, can't you?"

"No and neither are you. Let her have her night and let's stay out of it. We cooked up this scheme to get them together and now, it's up to them to decide what happens. We are lucky to have survived the night unscathed. I couldn't tell if they were mad or not. All I saw was them ogling each other every chance they got.

If they're knocking one out, good for them. We're not going to ask about that. From this point forward, we're going to mind our business. In fact, I've got some of your business I'd like to mind. I'm up, I'm picturing what I know is under that nightie you have on and I want it. It's not even cold in here, but you look quite perky on top! Come here, baby. Take your mind off of your sister and what she's doing and put it on what's under blanket number one!" he jested.

Renee dropped her head in defeat and knew that she was overreacting. Pulling the nightie over her head, she rolled to his side of the bed, reached beyond him to turn the light off and he stopped her.

"What? I'm naked," she cooed at him.

She loved that her life was never, ever boring with Fred, but sometimes understanding him took a little more patience than she sometimes had.

"Light on. I need to see you work it, baby."

"Then I'll call my sister if she hasn't called me by the time you pass out again. You know I got that touch," she boasted.

"Renee, if that phone rings and you stop to answer it, I'm calling my lawyer in the morning and I'm filing for divorce. If you attempt to make a phone call before the sun comes up in the morning and I'm not passed out because, well, you know how you can work a brother overtime, I'm going to take that phone, grab a hammer and smash it to pieces and then I'll buy you a new one, again, when the sun comes up. Your sister is fine. You and I would trust Keith with our lives and I have to say that setting them up to meet each other was the best idea you've ever come up with when it comes to setting people up."

"I did that, didn't I? I need to put up a sign and, like my mom always says, hang a shingle and start a new business around finding love for people," Renee joked.

"I wouldn't go that far, but I will say you have some loving right here in this room that needs your attention and your focus. No more talk of anyone else. You have some serious hooking up to do right here and right now."

Renee laughed and reached for his hands, raising them above his head. When he tried to move them to reach for her, she warned him.

"I won't reach for the phone and you will allow me to have my way and do whatever I want and you can't touch me. No matter how much you will want to and we both know you will, you're not going to," she ordered playfully.

She loved when they could play like this because the kids were gone for the night.

"Good and no more talk about your sister. If she's getting her freak on, I'm happy for her. I'd be much happier if we could stop all this talking, unless it's dirty, sexy talk."

"Dirty?" she asked, friskily.

"Real dirty," Fred groaned out.

"I got you, baby. Let me say this and I won't bring it up again tonight. If they hit it off and get married, I'm going to expect a big thank you speech at the reception."

"That's fine and I'll dance at her wedding with my two left feet. Speaking of dancing – since the kids aren't here, can I get the pole out, put it up and you can show me the latest moves that dance class has been teaching you?"

Renee giggled as she got off the bed, pulled the covers off of his body and pointed toward their closet where they kept a stripper pole which got a lot of use when the kids were spending the night away from home. Tonight, was a perfect night for it and she flopped back on the bed as soon as Fred jumped up and headed for the closet door.

"Grab the glass, high-heeled slippers and let me really show you my moves!"

"Pole dancing with nothing on but heels? Yes!" Fred declared.

When he reappeared looking like a kid on Christmas with everything they would need, excitement raced through her and nothing else other than her sexy husband was on her mind.

9

The night was unseasonably warm for it to be the Christmas season and because of that, Reagan strolled along with Keith, snug against him, her arm linked with his as if they were enjoying a bright, sunny, summer day.

"Dinner was amazing. I'll have to tell Fred that he was right. The crab cakes tasted as good, if not better, than any I could have in Maryland. The chef put his foot in them things and I could taste the fresh Old Bay seasoning. How was your fish?" she asked as they walked toward the hotel.

"It was delicious. Everything was perfect from the food to the company."

"I agree and the company was the best part. Imagine that," she said.

"Renee and Fred are so transparent and for once, I'm glad about it. You are one remarkable woman, Reagan Kelly."

She trembled, not against the mild weather, but in

acceptance of the piercing eyes that seemed to look deep into hers, reaching her soul. Over dinner, they'd shared their lives, their likes and dislikes. She enjoyed listening to him talk about how he crafted his storylines for his books. She knew how popular he was as a writer and to hear him talk about his family, especially his love for his sisters was admirable.

"So are you. I'm looking forward to enjoying the next couple of days."

"As am I. Is there anything as far as adventures that you don't enjoy doing?"

She thought and couldn't think of what type of adventures he was making reference to. She can't say that she was ever adventurous, though the idea appealed to her. She reflected on how boring her life really was. She had more fun as a young girl than she's had as an adult.

"Adventures like what? I don't know how to weigh that."

She could see in Keith's face that he was finding it hard to believe that she didn't have a more interesting life. It was clear over dinner that he was well traveled and loved mixing business with pleasure whereas, when she spoke about places she'd been, she couldn't even tell him about fun activities in the cities and countries that she'd traveled to. She had been all about business.

"For instance, if I found a place to go rock climbing or riding in a helicopter, does the idea frighten you or are you picturing that as something you'd love to try? Maybe you've tried both of those already," he said.

Keith was doing a lot of assuming. She hadn't done anything. Once she got to college and became career driven, she hadn't done much that wasn't related to work. Should she be embarrassed? She didn't know, but she felt comfortable being transparent with Keith.

"I'm open to both and anything else. My list of fun activities is very short – don't judge me. I guess I seem quite boring to other women you've been around? I heard you talk about all the places you've been and things you've done and how you encourage your sisters to live more. My sisters are like that with me, but I don't listen to them."

"I'm going to change that for you this weekend. There will be no judgement, no fear and you're going to have fun even if it kills us both. Well, maybe not to that extent, but you get the picture, right?" Keith laughed.

"I'm with you."

Reagan looked ahead and saw the lights of the hotel marquee in front of them, a sign that their night was just about over. For once, she was going to throw caution to the wind and see what she's been missing.

Images of Colin, Buster and even Ivan plagued her when she thought of how they saw her and played with her mind. She'd forgotten about Ivan, the man who'd played her for a fool.

Ivan Jacobs was the owner of a local Baltimore gym where she once worked out. She'd met him and realized she'd captured his eyes the first time she walked into the exclusive club to inquire about a membership. When one of the other members of the staff, Dawn, offered to give her the tour and answer all of her questions, Ivan appeared out of the shadows and took her place. They walked and he shared about all of the amenities of membership and how exclusive the club was. He personally accepted or denied membership based on the caliber of the person and if they could afford the high-priced membership.

After agreeing to the terms, he assigned himself as her personal trainer, something that came free for six weeks with a year-long membership. After a few weeks of working together, he'd asked her out and she was excited. She knew he was a busy person and that fit into how busy she was. What she didn't know was that his idea of a date was having her stay late at the gym and them having sex in his office. He would tell her that he liked her because she didn't require or demand a lot of his time and like him, she was a workaholic and understood the limits of their relationship. She thought she did, but she really didn't.

The sex with Ivan was so incredible, that days later, she would still be thinking about it and wanting more. What she hadn't thought about was the fact that they never went anywhere together, publicly. He would visit her condo, before she bought her house and they would stay in and relax, but only at late, late hours of the night. She would bring up meeting each other's families and he would get to the day of her meeting his family or him meeting her family and he'd have some kind of an emergency. She had been happy that she was involved with someone as gorgeous as Ivan with his exotic, island looks, that she didn't see a pattern.

Her wakeup call came when she had planned to meet him at the gym, but instead ended up having to work late. When she called to tell Ivan that she wouldn't make it, he told her to call him when she got home and he would come visit her. When her meeting ended up cancelled, she decided to surprise him at the gym. The moment she walked in, Dawn gave her a weird look and told her that Ivan said he wasn't expecting her. She felt Dawn's behavior weird when she asked if Ivan was in even if he wasn't expecting her. They were a couple and she didn't know what the hesitation was about.

Dawn's stuttering and looking around should have been her key, but that didn't happen. When a client asked Dawn a question, taking her away from the office, Reagan decided to go in search of Ivan. She walked into his office, something she did often and was planning on leaving her bag there and perhaps taking a shower with him later in his personal bathroom, down a private hallway from his office.

When she walked inside, she was about to turn around and find her favorite treadmill to start her workout when she could hear sounds coming from the hallway. Walking where she now wished she hadn't, she pushed slightly on the door to his private bathroom and caught sight of him in the shower and he wasn't alone. She started to storm in to demand an explanation, but Dawn grabbed her arm and pulled her back toward the office, leaving the sounds of sex in the shower behind her. She knew that sound; she'd been that woman.

"I'm sorry about that. I wanted to tell you who Ivan really was, but I didn't want to intrude."

Appalled, she looked to Dawn with tears in her eyes.

"Who he was? He's done this before?" she asked, a question she should have held on to and walked away, but no, she had to have an answer.

"All the time," Dawn said.

"Well, since when?"

Reagan regretted each question, especially her last one.

"Since before you and a lot after you. It's what he does. He's a sex addict, not a potential relationship. Most of the women who come through here are like you and that's why he accepted your membership."

"Like me? What does that mean?"

"He likes women who are dedicated to their

careers and are desperate for companionship when they have time. I'm sorry if that's offensive. Those are his words, not mine. He likes women who are inaccessible except for at night or when they need to be, shall I say, hit off? In other words, busy career women who don't make time for real relationship and of course, married women, like the one he's in there with now."

Each word from Dawn's mouth was like a knife to her chest.

"You knew and didn't say anything?" she bemoaned in embarrassment.

"I know and I'm sorry, but it wasn't my place. I have to work here and I stay in my lane. If it helps at all, I think that you're the first of his women that I really felt sorry for knowing he was messing around on you."

Reagan let out a deep breath of pain. There was that knife again.

"First of his women?"

Reagan let those words resonate as she grabbed her bag and walked out of the gym, never returning. She had her Sherry cancel her membership and to her surprise, Ivan never called to ask why or to even call just because. She was clearly more into him than he was into her.

Why she kept ending up with men like that, she didn't know. Keith, she could tell was different; at least she hoped so. He was certainly the first in a long time who convinced her that there was more to life than work and then proceeded to show her.

Putting her past behind her, she walked ahead of Keith as they entered the hotel and took the long escalator up to the bank of elevators that led to their floors.

They stood in silence as they waited and when she moved to pull her arm from being intertwined with his since they were no longer outside, she was surprised when he held her arm tighter and leaned closer to her.

"I enjoy having you close to me, if that's okay with you," he whispered.

Not only did she not mind, but she then gripped his arm tighter and smiled when he relaxed and caressed her hand.

When they stepped inside of the elevator car, he moved her arm down and took her hand in his, locking their fingers. They rode in silence.

Exiting, they walked toward her hotel room and paused outside of it.

"Well, this is my stop," she said turning to face him. "I had a great time with you tonight and, oh yeah, with my sister and Fred too, earlier," she joked.

When she looked into his eyes, something held her captive. She didn't know if it was his eyes, which were filled with mystery, the desire for her that she saw in them or the desire for him that first surfaced back at the concert.

"Tonight is the beginning of four remarkable days. I hope you're ready."

"I am."

"Do you mind if I check your room? I know if I wasn't with you that you'd be fine going into your room, but I would feel better if I made sure all was safe on the inside."

"Oh, that's fine. Fred usually does that when I come to visit them," she said. Handing him the card key to her room, she stood still as he entered and within a few seconds, came back out.

"All clear."

"Thank you for checking."

When she turned to enter her room, she felt Keith grasp her hand.

"Are you ready?" he asked slowly. To her, her ears heard him drawing out each word as if they were each their own sentence.

There was something about his words as a million different meanings flooded her brain. Her insides quivered with a longing for every meaning to come true; right now.

"For?" she asked brazenly. She knew he was probably making reference to tomorrow, but she was thinking more along the lines of being ready for him now. How desirous could one man be? Keith had surpassed her expectations in that area.

As his face came closer to hers, she sucked in a breath and prepared for whatever he was bringing.

She secretly hoped it would be more than just a hug good night.

"If I could walk away without just a small taste of your lips which have been calling out to me all night, I would but I'm not sure I can. Is that too much? Am I out of line?" he asked her pointedly – making sure there was no gray area.

Inside, she was doing a happy dance and even wondered if it was noticeable on the outside. She was full of excitement knowing she wasn't the only one thinking about how to end their first night together. A kiss would be perfect. A request to join her in her room, in her bed would better. She knew that was her lack of a sex life speaking, but Keith was a walking Adonis and she couldn't help herself.

As her stomach did flip flops all over the place as if she was about to be kissed for the first time, she moved closer to him, closing the space between them. The moment reminded her of the Will Smith movie, *Hitch* where he talked about how the moves to a kiss are made after the woman comes some of the way, the man should take that as a sign and come the rest of the way. She wasn't taking any chances on her desire for him being unclear.

As Keith angled his head and reached around to the back of her head to lightly hold her in an embrace under her long hair, her insides were fiery as his lips came down on hers, light at first and then she moaned, or was it him? She didn't care. She only wanted to feel and that's what she did.

Keith's lips were soft against hers and then she felt his tongue asking for entrance, to her delight. She really was doing a happy dance in her head now! When she opened for him and he deepened their connection, she gasped with joy at the cloud nine feeling her head was experiencing – a feeling that cascaded through her body, sending waves of want and pleasure everywhere.

When his other arm pulled her flush against his body, her entire being felt weightless as a kiss, like none other she'd ever experienced had her reaching around and holding on to him to keep from falling into a heap at his feet.

Her body's sensors were on overload as their tongues lapped and caressed, fueling their need for each other. She'd been in a constant state of heat since the second she'd seen him and the pressure of that feeling had her feeling like she was about to burst any second. The kiss was proof positive that their meeting, was meant to happen.

When Keith pulled away, ending the kiss, but not their connection, he looked as stunned as she felt.

"Woman, what are you trying to do to me. I knew the kiss would pack a wallop, but I wasn't ready for that much of a punch. Was that as good for you as it was for me?" he asked her and she laughed from her belly, trying to recall what movie that may have been a line from.

"It was better than good. I have a new love and respect for kissing," she admitted.

"Does that mean I'll be able to get another one before the end of the weekend?"

"Want one now?" she offered without thinking. She didn't know where the words have come from and she didn't care. Before she could think twice about it, he kissed her again and this time was better, and longer lasting than the first. If she was anywhere other than standing in the hall outside of her hotel room, she would have begun unbuttoning his shirt and his pants. She'd never wanted a man more which was crazy to her. She had just met him a few hours ago and yet, she felt as if her life would be empty without him.

Reagan wondered how crazy she would look if she broke out into her happy dance in the hallway. Containing her excitement and composure, she would wait until she was in her room alone to do that.

"Yes, I wanted another one now. I guess I should have answered before I kissed you," he said, breathlessly.

"Not necessary at all!" she proclaimed.

"There will be many more before Monday," Keith added.

"I certainly hope so."

"Thank you for tonight and especially for the kisses. I'll see you in the morning. Since you gave me your number at the restaurant, I'll ring your cell, but not too early. It's already late and I assume with you being on vacation and not having to get up early for work that you'd like to sleep in a little later than usual," he said.

Reagan's mind was screaming! She wanted him to call as early as possible. She couldn't wait to be in his company again and this time for a full day.

"I'll be up early and we can meet when you're ready; just call me."

"I will definitely do that. Go inside and lock the door before I walk away."

When she turned to enter her room, she felt his light touch on her arm. Before she could think, his lips met hers again, this time for a quick, soft kiss. It was fast, but just as powerful.

"I needed that to get me through the night. Til the morning, beautiful."

Reagan didn't know what to say. She was caught up in a cocoon and didn't want to come out or invite anyone else in other than Keith.

Going inside, she turned and waved as he winked just before she closed and locked the door behind her. Knowing she was alone, she finally did the happy dance that had been locked in her head all night long.

10

Reagan woke early Saturday morning with a big yawn and an even bigger smile. Had she really stayed up most of the remainder of the night before talking on the phone with Keith? She couldn't remember the last time she'd actually done that. Perhaps, not since her college days? She'd never been interested enough or found the time to have an all-night phone session, but that's exactly what she'd done after her night out for dinner. Lying flat on her back, she kicked her feet against the mattress again and again with pure happiness that it hadn't all been a dream; Keith was real and he was interested in her.

Had he really kissed the life out of her in the hallway? Stretching her arms and legs out even more, she added to the kicking by waving her arms in ecstasy over everything that was the day before. To say that she was thrilled that she hadn't gone back on her promise to Renee to come to New York was no way measuring how happy her day already was.

Sitting up on the side of the bed, she stood and

walked over to the large window that overlooked Time Square. Her day was filled with so many options to make the best of every moment. Today was more than just the next day; it was a new day; a new dawn. She thought back on the night before.

After grabbing a shower and getting ready for bed, she heard her cell phone ping and assumed it was Renee. To her surprise, it wasn't. It was Keith telling her that he couldn't think because his mind was filled with thoughts of her. He had asked if she was up for a quick phone chat or was she too tired and wanted to go to bed. She didn't answer by text. She dialed his number.

They had talked for two hours as if they hadn't just spent hours together. There was something about Keith that intrigued her and it was beyond his good looks and charming personality. He was genuine when he said he wanted nothing from her other than to show her a great and unforgettable weekend. How could she say no when she knew that his original plan had been to return to Baltimore but he instead, chose to stay a few more days, all because of her? Nothing and no one had ever made her feel as flattered as he had.

She'd been to New York quite a few times, either for work or to visit her sister and her family. Thinking of Renee reminded her that they were supposed to go shopping in a few hours.

Rushing back to the bed, she sat down on the

edge, picked up her phone and called her.

"You're just calling me? I was worried all night!" Renee yelled the minute she picked up.

"Liar! If you were up, you weren't worried about me. I assume any late-night activities for you would consist of Fred howling at the moon!" she joked.

"Real funny. You didn't think I would be worried about you in New York by yourself at that hour?"

"For starters, go into the kitchen and make a cup of coffee while we're talking because you are too on the edge this early in the morning. It's a beautiful day! I'm feeling great and I slept like a queen. Second, I was not out alone; I was with Keith. Remember him? You and Fred slyly set me up with him," she said.

"What? Who are you? You never wake up talking about anything being beautiful. What have you done with my sister? Are you a clone? Are you an alien inhabiting my sister's body? If so, be warned that you're going to be bored living as her.

Reagan would normally take a comment like that from Renee as criticism, but not this time. She was too good of a mood to be insulted.

"Haha, very funny. I'm having a good day."

"The question is, baby sister, did you have a good night and if so, how good was it? Was it rated G, R or X? No details needed, just tell me what kind of rating you would give your night so that I know my worrying was not in vain."

Reagan stood and danced around her room in her

Hello Kitty, two-piece satin pajamas and matching headwrap.

Throwing her body backward onto the bed, she smiled up at the ceiling as she took in everything from the night before and tried her best to relay it to Renee.

"Sissy, I wouldn't share too many details with you even though you aren't shy about what goes on between you and Fred. You are the queen of too much information sharing. My night out was G-rated. Who do you think your sister is anyway? You should not have been worried. If you didn't trust Keith, neither of you would have left me with him and went on about your merry little way, so stop the extra drama."

"Okay, you're right – I can't lie. He is great, isn't he? Just admit that. He's wonderful; damn near perfect!"

Reagan paused to let Renee suffer for a few countless moments.

"Yes, he is. I had the best time of my life last night and I will thank you after I berate you for setting me up like that as if I couldn't get my own date. You and Fred are foul for that and if this had turned out in any other way than absolutely fantastic, I would be hating on you right now, but I can't. I had an amazing time!"

"Okay, so tell me about it and what time are we going shopping? You can wait and tell me then. I want to hear everything except any seedy details. I had enough of your intimate life stories from your disappointing sex life with Colin. Why you even wanted to marry him, I don't get, but I digress. This isn't about him. Now, about Keith?"

"Oh, about the shopping thing; how mad would you be if I cancelled on you today? If you really had your heart set on us spending the day together, I can call Keith and cancel the wonderful day of unplanned activities we are going to have unless you're okay with me cancelling on you."

Reagan held in the chuckle she wanted to let out. She and Renee loved their usual tit-for-tat.

"I was all set to be mad about you cancelling until I heard Keith's name. As long as you're not cancelling because you suddenly realized you had work to catch up on, I'm all for giving Fred a break from the kids. They're coming home from spending the night with friends last night. He was going to take them out for the day while you and I were gone, but I'll reserve that for another day. You and Keith really hit it off, huh? Tell me while I'm making my coffee. You know it's early and I'm up alone. Spill!" Renee yelled.

Reagan laughed and did just that.

"Dinner was amazing. The food was so good and the crab cake was definitely from someone from Maryland. We arrived and got the perfect table. They weren't too crowded that late at night, but we tossed out Fred's name and got five-star treatment. There were some people who even recognized Keith and wanted his autograph. He asked me if I minded if he took a few seconds to do that, which I thought was considerate. Not many would do that. You know how famous people can be – all about them. We then ate and talked about all kinds of fun things, but nothing about work for either one of us. He told me about his family, his time in college with Fred, who I will kill for not telling me he knew Keith Jackson. I have many of his books and I plan to buy the rest this weekend so that I can have him autograph them. I learned a lot about his sisters and he spoils them rotten, sort of what you and Jen should be doing with me but don't quite get right. He talked about some places he's visited and others that he'd like to visit now that he's learning to slow down and enjoy each day."

"You could learn from that," Renee interjected.

"This is not your time to chastise me about my work ethic. I'm telling you about a man and you're taking digs at me. Not fair or cool, Sissy!"

"Whatever. What else."

"We sat until the restaurant closed and even though Fred had already paid for the night and from what I'm told, left a very large tip, Keith left a very nice extra tip for the staff. I don't how much it was, but let me tell you, I caught them dancing around in circles when they were told that he'd given them an extra tip on top of what Fred had already told the restaurant to take out. How selfless is that, especially when he didn't have to. Uh, what a man!"

"Don't say I never do anything for you!" Renee chimed.

"Whatever. Anyway, we left the restaurant and took our time strolling back to the hotel. He's staying here too, but you already knew that, right? Don't answer. He walked me to my room and checked it out before I entered. I forgot men actually do that kind of thing for women."

"That's because it's been ages since you've gone out on a date and even longer if it's with a real gentleman like him – a good guy."

"I can't argue with you on that, though I want to."

Reagan let silence live between them

as she thought of the weight of what Renee had just said. She really did struggle with dating, especially good dates.

"Are you still there? Is this thing on?" Renee hollered on the other end.

"Oh, yeah. Sorry. Where was I? Oh, right. We stood outside of my room and talked for a few minutes. He asked me if I was ready and I assumed he was talking about the fun stuff we're going to do today."

"Stuff like what? Where are you going?" Renee asked.

"I don't know. That's the fun of it all. If he wasn't someone you and Fred knew, I would be leery and get the scoop ahead of time, but he said we'll play it by ear. We'll be typical tourist and do whatever we want. I'm excited about the possibilities. This could be endless fun since there's so much to do in New York.

We could stop by your place later if you want me to. I know your plan was for us to spend some time together."

"Girl, please! I can do that anytime. How often does my baby sister get to spend the day with a hunky man as fine as Keith who appears to have eyes for you. I saw him eyeing you last night. He liked what he saw and he should have because you're beautiful. Go and have the time of your life and don't look back. Wait, he's not leaving today? I thought he had a flight out this afternoon?"

Reagan sat up and rocked from side to side, happy that Keith was willing to change his plans just for her.

"His was and he changed his mind. He's going to stay until Monday, the same day I'm heading back home."

"What!"

Renee screamed so loud, Reagan dropped her phone to the floor and had to quickly snatch it up.

"You heard me."

"So, does that mean you'll be spending more than just today with him?"

"Yes – the entire weekend and I'm excited. I would say I was so excited that I couldn't sleep, but I slept like a log for a few hours. We talked for two hours after he got to his room until neither of us could keep our eyes open any longer. I could have talked to him for two more hours. He's that engaging. We never lost things to talk about and the best part was, he loved listening to me talk about my life, the family and the things I want to do with my life. Other than you and Jen, I've never really shared that with anyone, not even my close friends. It came out naturally talking to him."

"Wow! Seems like the two of you really connected. I like what I'm hearing."

Reagan bit her bottom lip as she contemplated telling Renee about how the in-person part of their night ended.

"The kiss was out of this world, too. I've never been kissed so thoroughly before in my life! It was damn near erotic!" she shared.

"Wait, what? What did you say? He kissed you and you let him? It was good, huh? Damn, I'm jealous!"

"Liar, but I appreciate you saying it. It was magical. He was tender and the kiss was filled with so much passion that I came within seconds of inviting him inside my room. That kiss left me wanting everything that I've been missing. I mean, I've gone out with guys and been kissed and my sex life hasn't been too shabby, but it had been all about the motions and not the emotions before. The kiss with Keith was definitely filled with emotion; a desire that went beyond comprehension. He then kissed me quickly on the lips and told me to close the door and lock it. I wanted him to ask to come in, but then I didn't. I'm looking forward to having fun today, but you know I was thinking about how good the sex would have been. A woman can tell a lot about a man from a kiss," she offered.

"Don't I know it. You know how Fred and I met and how he laid one on me in an elevator. You see where that led – marriage, two kids and the best life a woman could have with an incredible man."

"You knew right away?"

Reagan had been second-guessing herself since Keith kissed her. Her history with men hadn't been the greatest. She questioned if she was about to enjoy a fun weekend only or if Keith was looking for more. She didn't know what she was in search of because once her life returned to normal, work would be the priority again and that's usually when men lose interest.

"I did and I know that sounds crazy, but it's true. Enjoy yourself. Enjoy him. Don't put too much pressure on yourself and for once, leave work in Baltimore. Don't talk about it, be about it or check on it. It will be there when you get home. Fred and I thought that you and Keith would like each other and we're not trying to marry you off. I just want you to experience the fun side of life. Fred had flown out to Los Angeles recently to meet with him and when he came back and mentioned that Keith was single and would be coming to New York soon, I thought it would be a good idea to introduce you. I kept it a secret because I knew you would fight me all the way. Have some fun and enjoy being with a man who I know will make sure you have an unforgettable time."

"What about after this weekend?"

"Live in the moment, Reagan. If you want more than this weekend, then you're bold enough to state that to him; I know you are. Don't lose your confidence when it comes to a man. Be you. If you only want this weekend, then have the best damn weekend possible. I think you'll begin to look at life differently, no matter what. I want you to be happy. Sometimes I don't feel like you want that for yourself."

"Sissy, I do want to be happy. I want to be happy like you and Jen are with your men. I can't seem to find my way to that. Do you think that maybe, I don't know how to be happy? Maybe I'm supposed to have these amazing achievements in work and let that sustain me."

After feeling so happy a moment ago, Reagan started feeling sorry for herself.

"Don't you dare do that to yourself. Don't you ever let me hear you feeling sorry for yourself as if all that you are is a working woman. Get yourself together, get dressed and go have a good time. Call me later. You and Keith be safe. I love you, Reagan. I love you so much! I could feel you smiling through the phone and that made me happy. Keep smiling!"

"I love you too, Sissy and thank you."

"Anytime, kiddo. Tell Keith I said what's up!"

Her phone pinged with a text message just as

their call ended. She scrolled through her phone and found it. When Keith's name appeared, her heart raced. Should she be this excited about a text message from a man she's only known one day? She read it and smiled.

"Ready for me? I mean for breakfast? I thought we could start the day at this place I love not far from the hotel. We can plan the rest of the day over omelets and home fries. Dress comfortably. You in?"

Reagan responded immediately.

"I'll be ready in fifteen minutes."

She jumped up, scanned the clothes she'd already hung up in the closet and found the perfect black and red sweat suit, red top and her favorite Nike Air Max 270 trainers in triple red. She wore heels so often that she didn't get the chance to wear sneakers often and was glad she decided to pack them for the weekend. Grabbing what she needed, she headed to the shower and found herself humming a tune to a song she didn't know and didn't care that she didn't know. She was already loving the newness.

11

If he could pat himself on the back for his expert level of multi-tasking, he would. Keith caught a glimpse of himself in the mirror as he slipped the jacket to his navy sweatsuit on over top of a pristine white t-shirt, ready for his day out with Reagan. It was early and he was glad that when he sent her a text, she was already up and just as ready as he was. While dressing, he was able to scroll through the tons of pictures his sister sent him of ideas for room colors in his condo and as he came across colors that were too bright for his taste, he called her and demanded changes.

"Change it Erika and I mean right now. Don't you dare put those colors anywhere in my place. I told you shades of blue in two of the bedrooms and black and white in the media room. I'd like gray and white in the kitchen and the same in the great room. Erin can have whatever colors she wants in the space that she's already claiming as hers, but if I see any red or burnt orange anywhere on the top level, I'm going to fire you."

"Keith, expand your mind. These are the it colors these days and I think it will look nice."

"Then have them in your house. Look, just stick with what we agreed upon and don't try to convince me to get these girlie colors. You know me better than that."

"What about when you get a wife? She won't want to live in this massive man-cave of dark, dull colors," Erika laughed.

"Well, if and when I do, she can redecorate however she chooses, but until then, no girlie colors.

"When you get back later today, I'm going to show you the actual colors against your wall and trust me, you're going to call me an amazing person for livening up your life. I came all the way from California to do something with your empty space and you don't appreciate it. I'm hurt, big brother."

"I doubt if seeing them in person will make me change my mind and I'm not coming back today. I'll be there on Monday, maybe Tuesday at the latest."

"Why? When we talked last week, you were sure you'd be back today, Saturday. What happened?"

"What's the big deal? It's only two or three extra days. Were you planning to head back west before then?"

"No. I'm here for two weeks to fix your undecorated life. I was hoping to get the painting started this weekend and I don't want to pick something you'll hate once you see it. What do you have, extra meetings?"

"Look, I have to jet. I'm meeting someone for breakfast and I don't want to be late."

Grabbing his room key and wallet, Keith rushed out of his room to be sure Reagan didn't arrive in the lower lobby without him being there to greet her, hopefully with a kiss as powerful as the one the night before. He went to bed thinking and thankfully, dreaming about that kiss and her soft, supple, very kissable lips. The way she kissed him back with such vigor had him thinking twice about spending the rest of the night alone. He'd met plenty of women in his life, but not one of the women in his past had him hemmed up as fast as Reagan has mesmerized him. When he kissed her, he saw the future and it included the two of them loving, living and raising kids together. It happened in a split second and that was all he needed.

"What?" he shouted into the phone as he walked.

"Never mind. You're distracted which means it must be a woman. Tell me I'm lying. It's a woman, right? Is she beautiful? Can I meet her? Send me her picture and a name so that I can google her."

"You will not google her and I'm not sending you anything," he kidded.

"Ah, it is a woman. I knew it! Is she special or is she as temporary as your idea that you won't like a red accent wall in your media room?"

How his sister was able to combine their

conversation about a woman with his desire of no red in his place astounded him. He loved both of his sisters but Erika had a way of pushing all of his buttons.

He didn't answer her though he already knew Reagan wasn't meant to be temporary in his life.

"I'll be back on Tuesday and she's not temporary, if I have anything to say about it and that's the end of the conversation."

"Call your agent. Your assistant dropped off some packages you've been waiting on and he said Carl has been blowing up his phone hoping someone would put him in direct contact with you. You're ignoring your agent these days? She must be some woman!"

"She is and I'll call him. I forgot I had a meeting set up with him later today that I need to cancel. In fact, I'm not dealing with anything that relates to work of any kind until I leave New York."

"Can I meet her?"

"I'll let you know. I need to call Carl. Anything else?" he asked as he reached the lobby and looked around for Reagan.

"No. Have fun and it's good to see you having a life outside of books and movies. I love it and I love you, big brother. I'll see you on Tuesday."

"Cool. No red, Erika. Bye," he said ending the call and immediately dialing his agent. He expected push back on his date for heading to Baltimore, but he was ready. His only priority would soon meet him for breakfast. He wasn't surprised when Carl answered on the first ring.

"Carl, I know you're pissed that I didn't call you back after the million times you called me yesterday. Just letting you know that I won't be back until Monday, sometime in the evening."

"Keith, you were supposed to come back today. I scheduled a meeting about a book tour with a promoter after the sit down meeting you and I were supposed to have. I flew into Baltimore specifically for the meeting with you."

Everyone wanted a piece of him, but he wasn't going back on his plans with Reagan.

"I will, of course, cover the cost of your hotel and flight and if you can't stay until I come back, I understand; we can reschedule or do a conference call. There is a change in my plans," he explained.

"I know you have a lot going on with the movie you're doing, but you also said you wanted to tour for the next year, especially with the new series you're releasing early next year. The upcoming holiday season will be prime for promoting the series and we need to work on the game plan."

Keith looked around the lobby of the hotel, hoping to catch Reagan as she came down the escalator. He thought about stopping inside of the Starbucks inside of the hotel and grabbing them two cups of coffee, but decided to wait until they were eating breakfast. He was able to snatch up a few brochures from the concierge to check into activities going on around town.

"No can do. I know what I said, but my plans have changed."

"I can find things to do in Baltimore until you return, buddy, but listen, I went through a lot to get you this meeting and the money that's being offered is stupid crazy!"

"Carl, you know it's not about the money. I have a lot of it and so do you. I have something else that I need to give my attention to and that means a few extra days in New York. Try and reschedule for later in the week."

"What about the interviews? You're scheduled to record two interviews with national news channels. We need to prepare for those," Carl said.

"I'm going to need you to exhale and deal with this. Neither one of us is new to this and it will all workout. You really need to relax more. I'm trying to. Why do we need to prep? I know all there is to know about every single one of my books and the idea behind the movies are mind and Fred's and we know it from the beginning to the end. There's no need to worry. You said you were bringing Phoebe with you to Baltimore and if that's the case, take your woman out and get away from work for a few days. That's what I'm about to do."

"Ah, it's a woman that's got your mind off of work. I thought you were hanging out with Fred for a day after your meetings. Sounds like more than that. What gives?" Carl asked.

Keith was about to respond and then he saw Reagan wave at him from the top of the long escalator.

"Fred introduced me to his sister-in-law and all I can say is there isn't anything more important to me right now than taking some time and getting to know her. I'm hanging up now, Carl, and don't call me until Tuesday. I'm going to send my assistant a text and have him book me on a flight out sometime Monday afternoon."

"Wait...but..."

Keith cut him off.

"I mean it Carl, no calls, no texts, no emails that have anything to do with business."

He smiled when he heard Carl huff on the other end. He knew the conversation was over.

"I got you. Have fun and I'll talk to you Tuesday. Don't go off and get married or anything like that. It could ruin your image as one of the sexiest men alive. Remember the *People Magazine* article on you?"

As Reagan stepped off the escalator, he walked in her direction.

"If you were looking at the gorgeous woman that I'm looking at, you wouldn't make any promises and neither am I. Bye, Carl."

"Good morning."

Leaning back, he looked in her eyes and then whispered.

"A very good morning it is. You look beautiful and comfortable."

"I feel both and I'm starving."

"That's good because I love a woman with a hearty appetite. You'll love the food. Shall we go? It's only a few blocks away from here. I make a point of eating there every time I'm in New York," he said, taking her hand in his and heading toward the revolving door.

"I thought maybe you were talking about Juniors Restaurant across the street," Reagan said.

"Oh, I love the food there also, but this morning, I'm taking you to a very small, quaint restaurant that has seating where you're almost on top of each other, but trust me the food is delicious. Have you had the cheesecake from Juniors?"

"I have and I love it."

"Good to know. I'd like to buy you a slice later when we return to the hotel."

"That sounds like a plan. What else are we doing today?"

Keith's mind was all over the place. As he guided them through the throngs of people on the street, he could think of a lot of things he'd like to do, but he wanted the plans for the day to be made together.

"I picked up some information on a lot of things we could do. We can rent bikes, go ice skating someplace, go to the American Music of Natural History, since we are both history buffs."

"We did share a lot didn't we. I've never met

anyone into history as much as I am. I hated getting off of the phone when we started talking about the sinking of the Titanic. I never tire of talking about that," she said.

"Me either. I have a book I want to recommend to you on that very topic. It's full of interviews with survivors that were conducted shortly after they were rescued. It's fascinating to me and I think it will be to you too."

When he watched her come down the escalator in her sweat suit, black leather bomber jacket and bright red sneakers, his mouth went dry. Her hair had been pulled up with a tie at the top of her head and her long twists sat high on her head, showing more of her beautiful facial features. She had on light makeup and her full lips popped with a beautiful shade of burgundy lipstick, which was a sexy contrast to her light skin. His body leaped with desire at the notion of kissing the lipstick from her lips without caring that it would end up on his lips. He welcomed it.

As they walked, he tried to think of anything other than how much he wanted her. He wanted to get to the fun part before thinking about adult fun they could share together later if she was up for it. He definitely was; he'd been up for it all night as they talked.

"Maybe we can stop at a bookstore later today and I can see if they have it. I spend so much time running around doing all kinds of other things that I don't take the time to actually go into a bookstore anymore, preferring to save myself the time and just order what I want online. I miss bookstores. You would be pleased with the large library I have at home."

Keith looked over and down at her as they walked with her hand in his.

"Maybe I'll get an invitation to check it out one day," he uttered and didn't wait for an answer as they crossed the street once the light changed. He wanted the idea of it to live in the air between them.

"What else is on tap for today? Are you sure you have the whole day free? I don't want to keep you from anything."

"Reagan, I have no place else I would rather be than hanging out with a beautiful woman on a beautiful day. There are lots of festival we can go to and eat until we pop at the many food trucks and of course there are plays and other concerts on and off-Broadway."

Keith opened the door to the restaurant in the middle and was happy that they were able to get a table immediately. That wasn't always the case since it was small, yet very popular.

"What do you recommend? It all looks delicious."

"Try an omelet and the home fried potatoes. If you like onions, get tons of those. You'll love it. We can also share a pancake. When you see the size, you'll know why. It's a lot for one person."

"That's a lot of food!" Reagan laughed.

"Is that too much food? I wasn't sure if you like a big breakfast in the morning. They also have lighter options on the menu if you would prefer that. I can point out a few."

"And miss the potatoes and pancake? Not on your life. I'm not one of those salad and fruit eating kind of sisters. I stay in shape because I work out, but I am a foodie and breakfast is my favorite meal of the day. I often pig out on omelets and pancakes."

"That's what I'm talking about. No judgement here. Eat whatever makes you happy. I love a woman who enjoys good food and you can't come to New York and not expect to indulge in some good food."

"I'm all for that. I don't want you to be shocked at the number of hotdogs I buy from the carts on the street today. I won't be mad if you have to turn your head in shame, but I'm going to eat and eat. Now, about the information you have on activities. I want to do everything."

"Everything it is."

Keith pulled out the brochures from his jacket pocket and shared a few with her while he looked at two others. When she was looking down, he looked over at her and silently thanked Fred and Renee for introducing them. He remembered sharing with Fred during one of his other recent trips to New York that he found it hard to date when women knew who he was. Sometimes, they had ulterior motives that were beyond just wanting to be with him as Keith, but with

Keith Jackson, the famous crime novelist. Reagan didn't care about any of that. They had a full day together ahead of them and by the end of it, he had a feeling their lives would be changed forever.

12

"Did you have fun today?" Keith asked her as they entered the roundabout full of elevators at the hotel.

"Do you see all these bags in my hands and this big smile on my face? This day was perfect!" she proclaimed. "I can't remember when I've ever had this much fun. We have been out all day. This is a record for me!" Reagan added.

"I'm happy to hear that and can I bribe you to never tell anyone that you saw me fall on ice skates. It was my first time, but I'm still supposed to be cool and if I fall, I'm supposed to do it all masculine like. I don't think that's what happened though. A seven-year-old girl had to help me up," he joked.

Reagan doubled over and laughed so hard that she dropped one of her bags. When Keith tried to bend down and help her, he ended up dropping the two bags of books that he was carrying for her. They ended up falling to the floor together in a mutual fit of uncontrollable laughter.

"Now, you've fallen twice in one day and I'm telling everybody!" Reagan declared.

"How about I buy you dinner as a bribe and you promise to never speak of this or me falling on the ice. My image is at stake here."

"It's a good thing we came back when we did. I don't think we would have made it far with all of these books," she said.

"Did you leave any in the store? Are there no bookstores in Maryland at all?"

"I know and I felt bad at first, but then I realized I needed them all, especially the few of yours that I didn't have."

"I would have given you those. You didn't have to buy them. I have tons at home."

"But you wouldn't have gotten a record of the sale if you give them away. I'm happy to support you as an author and I wouldn't have it any other way. I do expect an autograph since I have an in with the writer. I hear he's great," she said.

When the correct elevator door opened, they jumped in with lots of other people and were crammed in the back. Reagan was about to speak when Keith leaned close to her ear.

"If I forget to say this later, you have made my day. I haven't had this much fun in ages, just like you."

"Then this was a great day for us both to let our hair down."

"Are you too tired for dinner? We didn't eat and we didn't get our cheesecake."

Reagan wanted dinner and dessert, but after a day of being flattered and complimented by Keith, she was hoping for some alone time and confident or not, she had no idea of how to broach the subject. She didn't want him to think the worst of her. She wasn't thinking in terms of sex, but just in relaxing with her feet up and enjoying each other's company. The combination of New York, no work and a gorgeous man was bringing out the romantic side of her that had been dormant for far too long. What she really wanted was more of his hot, spicy, steamy kisses like the one they shared the night before. If what she was being offered was dinner and cheesecake, she'd take that too.

"Both sound great. What did you have in mind?" she asked.

"Would I be too forward if I invited you to dinner and cheesecake in my suite? We've been out all day and we could have a do-nothing night of relaxing, watching movies, order us some dinner and have dessert delivered from across the street. If I'm out of order, I apologize, not for asking, but for assuming it would be okay. I had fun today, but I'd really like to spend some time alone with you, no strings, I promise."

"No strings at all? Suppose I wanted a string or two? I'm not talking about forever, but if we're going to explore the weekend and just live in the moment, I'd really like some alone time with you also."

She started to say more, but the elevator reached her floor. Neither of them moved. Instead, they turned and faced each other and with no one around them, Reagan sighed in relief that they could talk freely.

"We are having a no limit to fun kind of weekend, but there will be limits that you'll set. I'm going to follow your lead," Keith said.

Reagan again found her confidence.

"What if I wanted just this weekend and a little more than dinner and dessert? Do I sound slutty or anything?"

"The weekend is all you want? What about after the weekend? We both live in Maryland. Are you saying you wouldn't want to consider more between us than this weekend?" he asked her.

"I don't know. I know what my life can be like and it's not the perfect set-up for more. I'm really enjoying time with you and I know it's only been two days. I don't want either of us to set any expectations. I like you; I'm having fun and I have to admit that after that kiss last night, I've been thinking about the images the kiss left me with."

"You don't sound slutty and never think that. You sound like a woman who knows what she wants, at least for the weekend and I'm fine with that. We both live busy lives and maybe thinking about more than this weekend is more than either of us can actually offer. I'd like to, but I don't want to pressure you into anything either. Down for that?"

"Yes, I am down for that. I want to grab a few things from my room, if that's okay with you," she said as they walked into her room.

"Anything for you."

Having Keith in her space, in her room where was a bed was a bit overwhelming. She looked around aimlessly as if she couldn't remember what she needed. The man looking and smelling good was first on her list.

"What did I come in here for? I can't remember," she mumbled.

"Can I ask you a question about tonight?"

When Keith's hand came out and reached for her, she moved and sidled up to him where he stood, leaning against the wall near the dresser.

"Yes," she replied softly.

"Spend the night with me."

Reagan's insides were singing a praise, but she held her composure.

"Are you sure?"

"I've never been surer of anything in my life. I'm asking now because I want you to get what you'll need for the night. We can always come back if you find you left something."

"I'd like that. Let me get a bag and put some stuff in it."

"Do you need to call your sister? I know you haven't spoken to her since we had lunch earlier today."

"I'll text her after we get to your room."

"Are you going to tell her you're spending the night with me?" he asked.

Reagan had been thinking the same thing. There was no doubt Renee was someplace at home waiting by the phone for details on how her day went. She didn't mind sharing that, but what she hoped was about to happen between her and Keith, she wasn't planning on sharing any details before or after.

"No. Will you tell Fred?"

"This is between me and you and no one else. I know they're waiting to see if their plan worked, but I keep my very private life, very private. What we share is only for me and you."

When Keith's head lowered toward hers, she grasped his arms a little tighter and as their lips touched lightly at first, she released a sexy mewl on the stimulating feeling of his lips against hers. Like last night, the feel of him brought on an anticipation for the kind of attention from a man that she's been craving, but hasn't been getting.

When he kissed her silly yet again, there was an unspoken statement of what she could expect before the end of the night.

When they separated, she tried to wipe away the lipstick that now covered Keith's lips. When he swatted her hand away and laughed, she left it where it was.

"You're going to look strange on the way to your room with my lipstick covering your lips."

"Baby, I don't care anything about that. Everyone who looks at me is going to be jealous knowing that the sexy woman I'm with planted one hell of a kiss on me! Get what you need and I'll sit right here and wait. Besides, I need to sit so that the embarrassing nature that rose from the kiss isn't as obvious as it is with me standing here in front of you.

Reagan tried to not look down, but curiosity won out and she was glad it had. Her eyes had to be deceiving her or she was in for a real big treat!

"Whew! Let me hurry up!" she exclaimed and rushed into the bathroom to grab toiletries to put in her bag and then a thought came over her. Turning she ducked her head back out of the door.

"Something wrong?" Keith asked.

"Um, I wasn't planning on anything and I, um, am not really prepared, if you know what I mean."

"I do. Don't think that I'm usually flying around with condoms in my luggage. I got up very early this morning and made a run to the store. After last night's kiss, I didn't want to be caught off-guard if you were as turned on by that kiss as I was. We're good on that front if that's what you were alluding to."

"Add to your resume that you're a mind reader!"

**

157

Keith walked ahead of Reagan into his suite and watched as she looked around at the difference in their rooms.

"Wow! I'm going to need my sister to up her game when it comes to my accommodations when I visit her. This is amazing."

"It's the presidential suite and I love the all-around view of New York City."

"What an incredible view!"

"My view is better."

"You make me feel so warm inside. I've never been as transparent with anyone like I've been with you. I actually rode in a helicopter today; me, timid Reagan rode in a helicopter and I loved it. I can't believe that at thirty-two years old, I still have so many things I'm just learning how to do that are fun. I grew up having money and could travel and pretty much do anything I wanted to do and yet, I haven't. Until now, I didn't know what I was missing.

"Thankfully, there is still time to see and do whatever your heart desires."

Moving away from the wall, he walked over and pulled her into his arms.

"I feel new when I'm with you," Reagan mumbled.

Keith felt her trembling in his arms.

"There is much more to come; tonight and tomorrow."

"I'm looking forward to tonight."

"Before we get comfortable and put everything out

of our minds other than each other, tomorrow – do you swim? I have access to a private pool for you and me only."

"I love to swim. Can you swim?"

"I'm an expert swimmer. I actually swam on my college team for my last two years and then bigger dreams took over."

"I'd love to go swimming. I even bought a few suits with me from home."

"I don't know if my heart will be able to handle seeing your gorgeous body in a swim suit."

"Well, get your heart ready because one is a very sexy white two-piece."

"My heart will have all night to prepare and I think after tonight, I'll be ready to see you in everything, anything and especially nothing."

"I like the sound of that."

"Is it hot in here to you?" he asked.

"I don't know about you, but I'm burning up."

"You're not alone, sweetheart. I'm going to order us some food and we're going to get comfortable and relax. We have all night," he moaned against her lips.

"Do you mind if I take a shower?" Reagan asked.

"Take anything you want. The world is yours."

"Well, in that case – can I take a shower and take you with me?"

"Mmm, a woman who knows what she wants and when."

Keith slid his jacket off and reached for the hem of

his shirt, pulling it over his head. Unexpectedly, he felt Reagan's warm lips caress and then kiss his chest and a sexy tremor raced through his body.

"Your every wish is my command," Keith said, taking her by the hand as they walked together toward the shower and toward the start to a beautiful night.

**

A satisfying stretch, a slight yarn and arms holding her tight in an embrace was how Reagan dreamed of waking up in the morning, though it wasn't quite morning. She smiled to herself and caressed Keith's arm which was wrapped around her waist. His breath blowing lightly in her ear was as arousing as the way he touched, caressed and kissed her into submission throughout the night. Her womanhood tingled with remembrance.

Slipping out of his embrace, she slid out of bed, careful not to wake him and using the bright, New York City lights outside of the window, she slipped on her pink, satin robe, tying the sash around her waist to cover her nakedness. There was something about the city being opened all night long that enticed her to the window where she looked from one bright neon display to the next. This is what she knew she'd been missing for far too long; enjoyment of the moment. In general, life passed her by so quickly that she often forgot to just stand still and just be.

Her night with Keith, more enjoyable than she'd ever experienced was the kind of loving that could sustain a woman for life. Pulling her robe tighter as she thought back to how intense he loved and how he made her body sing like never before, she exhaled, expressing the joy of how her life changed in two short days. How could she have lived so long and never put her needs first?

"Why are you awake?"

Turning slowly at the sound of Keith's magnetic voice, she leaned back against the window and allowed her eyes to focus on the sight before her of a man, in all of his glory, a view of pure perfection. She could see his arm above his head as his hairy chest peaked out at her like a charmer zoning in on her heart, causing it to beat at a rapid pace, her desire for him all-consuming even after the multiple times he'd already brought her to climax in one night. If she were counting, she would start at four and knowing the night wasn't over yet, she was looking forward to adding to that number.

"I couldn't sleep. I didn't want to miss any part of this peacefulness. I never get this. I never experience this."

Keith got out of bed, still completely naked and walked over to her – her eyes taking in every exposed part of him. Her mouth watered and her legs twitched. How could a man be this virile even in the darkness with only his outline being clear?

When he turned her in his embrace until she was again facing the outside world, she leaned into his embrace. Even now, she could feel him hardening against her back, loving their closeness as much as she was. They were so in-tuned, it was frightening. Could she be safe in hoping for more than just this unforgettable weekend? Was she allowed to have more than her previous mere existence? Should she try to have more?

"You have to learn to refocus your wants and needs. I get that you love work and you feel obligated because as the saying goes, to much is given, much is required. Baby, you really can have what you want and not just what's expected."

"You make me want more than that."

"I want you to want more than that, not for me and not because of me, but because you see yourself having more. All you have to do is reach out for it, grab it and make it yours. What do you want?"

When Keith's lips caressed her neck, she leaned her head further to the left to give him even more access. His touch was rich and filled with emotion and she'd be crazy to deny that she wanted as much of him as she could get. She turned around and faced him, wrapping her arms around his neck as much as she could. When kissed her slow, thoroughly and methodically, she tried to climb up his body. She didn't want to talk anymore, she only wanted to feel.

"You," she whispered against his soft lips. "I just want you."

As Keith untied the sash around her robe, she

thought he was removing it, but instead, he opened his hand where he'd been holding a gold pack and tore it open with his teeth, keeping his eyes locked on hers. Her breath hitched when she felt him long, hard and strong against her stomach as her desire grew to an altitude not reachable by the human flesh.

"Yes, I have a condom in my hand. When I woke up and saw you standing at the window, a vision of beauty, I felt a delectable longing to get back to that place where neither of us needs to think; we only need to feel."

With protection in place, she went into his arms as he lifted her against the glass. She didn't feel the coldness of it against her back through the robe. Her body was giving off too much heat to even know it was a cold, winter night. Locking her legs around his waist, she leaned her head back against the glass and Keith used his free hand to open her robe even more, where his eyes and lips focused on her breasts.

When his lips circled and then closed over one hard nipple, she shrieked with the bliss of a woman who was having every craving fulfilled. She heard her own breathing in the quietness of the room, with the only other sound being Keith's moans of pleasure. She loved the freedom of not having to be in control, especially when it came to lovemaking. She was used to being in total control of every aspect of her life that relinquishing it to someone else, was freeing.

As his mouth traveled to the other side of her

chest, she felt the pull between her legs while moving her hips up and down, feeling him grow even harder against the area between her legs that was, without a doubt, completely drenched.

"I need you," she uttered, not shy about every need she had; the greatest of need being him.

"I'm right here, baby. I'm right here for you. Hold on," he groaned into her ear and she held his shoulders tighter. In the next second, she felt him; she felt his hips moving forward, slowly, grinding against her with precise, circular movements. As her head flailed from side to side, unbeknownst to her until this weekend, when she focused on the moment, she could have an out of body experience, like she was now. She could see herself enjoying being pleasured and nothing else existed. She felt the fire burning hot through her as every nerve ending in her body was on high alert. She was high on desire.

"Yes," she crooned into Keith's ear as he moved inside of her with determined strokes with her own matching him move for move.

"This – us is pure perfection. Do you feel it?" he hummed.

"Yes, yes."

"This is us, baby. This is us after two days. This kind of feeling isn't something that everyone experiences. This is once in a lifetime. This is unforgettable."

When she wanted to respond, she couldn't. With a

quickness, Keith stole her breath away when his body surged powerfully into hers, his hands now gripping her behind, protecting it from the friction against the glass. Feeling him with his thickness going into her until there was no more room and them pulling out to the tip, only to flow back in, stole every part of her being and she loved it. She loved feeling vulnerable and alive. She loved their oneness, a connection with someone that she never knew was possible.

She rode him and he loved her powerfully as their loud breaths and the delightful sound of their lovemaking where their bodies joined in luscious delight was all she needed and then it happened. Her body rose higher and higher as she bounced harder, pushing forward as he pressed forward and up and then she lost all control. Lights, brighter than those outside of the window flashed before eyes as her release slammed into her again and again.

"Keith!" she screamed, unable to be silent and not caring if the whole world could hear her.

"I'm with you, baby – I am right there with you!" he shouted.

From their dual moans to the drunk like, tipsy like feeling she was indulging in caused the moment to turn into a lover's musical as the sound playfully stroked her ears, driving her wild with her desire to go even higher. Keith's loud, powerful groans of his own release spoke to her body and her heart as she held him close, trying to be the strength she knew he needed when his herculean body movements and groans turned to animalistic growls. Together they soared with a passion that was reserved only for them. He was right, this was perfection.

13

"Renee, can you stop fussing at me long enough to listen to me explain? I know I was late meeting you at the gym this morning, but you have no idea what I left in bed or should I say who. I wouldn't leave a bed with a man as sexy as Keith in it for anyone other than you. Why are you still fussing? Isn't this what you wanted from me? You set this up for me to have a fun weekend and when I accept your challenge, you want to fuss. Being angry this early in the morning is usually my job and it's usually aimed at you, not from you," Reagan laughed.

"It's Monday and I haven't seen you since Friday. You spent all day and night with Keith Saturday and Sunday and all I get on Monday morning before you're scheduled to take the train back home is a meager hour of your time. If I wasn't so happy for you, I would be genuinely upset with you, but I can't. Let me have this one second to be upset that you ignored me all weekend and then I promise to be happy for all the hot, sexy fun you've been having. You could have, at least, had breakfast with me since I was able to rework my schedule to go into the flower shop later than usual this morning."

"I called you several times this weekend and asked if you wanted me to come by and you told me to keep having fun and that's what I did. Yesterday got away from me. We got up early to go stand at the window outside of the weekend Today Show. You know I've always wanted to do that and for a long time, that was shut down. If you watched the show, you may have seen me. Keith then took me to an outside concert, which I thought would be awkward since the weather was colder, but I loved it. He even took me on an hour-long horse drawn carriage ride around the city. Then, last night, on a Sunday night, get this – we went to a nightclub and I danced like I've never done before. I barely sat down except for when I needed to drink water to hydrate. This weekend was amazing for me, but go ahead and holler at me. I cannot make you happy," she quipped.

"I'm over the moon with happiness for you. You visited monuments I've never been able to get you to do with me on the few visits you've made to New York over the years. You've having all this amazing sex, and I know you have even if you don't give me the down and dirty details. I wanted to hear more, I guess. I need more!"

Reagan laughed as she raced around her room,

rushing to pack so that her luggage would be ready when it was time for her to leave later in the day. She was hastening to get to her last few hours with Keith. They were doing a little more shopping and of course, a late lunch at their now favorite breakfast spot.

"You're not getting more. Just know that when I say it was a struggle to get out of his bed this morning, knowing what I was leaving behind all naked and ready for more, I need you to be appreciative and not fuss. I promise to come back for a visit soon and I'll make it all about you!"

"You better. Does this weekend mean you're going to pursue more with him when you get back home? He's right there in Baltimore, arms-length away; I'm just saying."

"I want to. When I left his room early this morning to get back to mine to change and meet you, he said he wanted to talk to me about something that would take more than a few minutes. I can see myself in something long-term with him, if that's what he wants. Can I tell you something without you judging me?"

"With me, you will always have a no-judgement zone unless you turn back into a workaholic and in that case, all bets are off because I'll be judging you day and night," Renee joked.

"Whatever. So, here it is. Am I crazy to say I think I've fallen in love with Keith? That's crazy, right? I mean, a woman doesn't fall in love with a man after a few days of hanging out and having the best sex of her life. It can't be love; it must be the good sex. I've never felt so alive. I feel like I want to write poetry all day and let out all this love I'm feeling for him. I mentioned a few places I've always wanted to visit like Maldives, Paris, Rome, Barcelona, Tokyo and so many other places and not for work. His response was that I should go to all of those places and maybe we should go together."

"What? He said that? What did you say in response?" Renee asked.

"I didn't respond. I just smiled over at him and changed the subject."

"No, Reagan."

"That's it. All you have to say is no Reagan?" she asked.

"You can have this. You know that, right? You can have that travel kind of life on beaches around the world sipping some fruity drink during the day and having a man love all on you at night. You can go anywhere you want to go. You have plenty of money – more than you'll be able to spend in a lifetime. I bet you haven't even touched your trust fund that grandpa left you. Don't answer, because I know you haven't. You have invested well and have had money invested for you and the dividends are huge from that. I know what your yearly salary is and from that alone, you can live any kind of life you want. You can take time and travel and do it with a gorgeous man who is probably just as much in love with you as you are with him. Stop cutting yourself short and just live; live your way."

"What's wrong with me that I can't stop questioning my right to happiness? Why can't I allow myself to be happy? How can I just be okay with having an unforgettable weekend with an amazing man and not want to have it forever? I know I want it, but where is that part of me that knows I deserve it? I want him, Sissy. I really do."

"Then tell him. Don't you dare leave New York without telling him how you feel and that you want to see where things can go with starting a relationship with him. You will find that you'll see a new normal and it will include Keith. From what you told me this morning about the past few days, you were not in that alone. If all you ask him for is this weekend, then that's all you'll have if you aren't honest with yourself and especially with him."

Reagan stood feeling renewed. Her sisters gave her advice often, but today, she felt empowered to go for what she wanted and that was a life with Keith beyond the weekend. The setup was perfect with them living in the same town. She saw many sleepless nights in her future, dates and romantic vacations.

"You're right."

Reaching over, she turned on her work cell phone for the first time in three days as she listened to Renee encourage her to finally get what she wants out of life while letting everything else take a second seat.

"You hear me?" she heard Renee ask.

"I missed what you said, sorry. I turned on my other cell phone and daddy has been blowing up my phone for the past hour with calls. I better call him back."

"No work, Reagan!" Renee shouted at her.

"I know, I know. I'm going home in a few hours and maybe he's checking to see if I've had a good weekend. He wasn't happy about me taking four days off, but once he hears about the great time I had, he'll be happy I took the time off."

"From your lips to God's ears. Daddy will always think about work first and everything else second, but go ahead and call him. Call me when you get to the train station and when you arrive back in Baltimore. Even though I didn't get to see much of you, I'm glad you came. This happy, smiling and giggling like a school girl Reagan is exactly who I wanted to see. I love you. I see daddy is now blowing up my cell phone, since I'm on the house phone talking to you. You call him first since he's probably checking to see why you haven't called him back. I'm sure that's why he's calling me. I love you and remember this weekend and all that your life can be after this moment. It's all in your hands. You have the power to get what you want and that means Mr. Sexy, Keith Jackson."

"I love you too, Sissy. I'll call you later and thanks.

I needed this weekend."

With that being the end of the conversation, Reagan ended the call and immediately dialed her father, surprised that he picked up before she even heard the dial tone. She was ready to dive right in to tell him about Keith.

"Hey, dad! Good morning! How are you? Are you calling to check-in to make sure I'm having a good time? I can't wait to tell you about my fun weekend and let me just say it was amazing. Wait until I tell you about..."

Her words were paused when he cut her off.

"You should be here at the bank. There's a lot going on. We are in crisis mode and you're off gallivanting in New York City. Everyone is here and ready to manage what's going on and I need you here. This is just terrible; just terrible. We have a lot to do. Are you back? Are you on your way back? Can you get here in a few hours? I need you; we all do. The staff is having a hard time with this."

Reagan stood suddenly after hearing the panic in his voice. What was he talking about that everyone was having a hard time dealing with?

"Dad, what are you talking about? What's going on?"

"You haven't heard? Have you not been watching the television or in contact with your staff? Sherry hasn't called you? What have you been doing that you're not connected to what's going on at the bank?"

Reagan exhaled and scrolled through her work phone and saw text after text and un-listened to voicemail messages from Sherry, others on her team and even a friend who works for one of the local Baltimore news networks. Something was definitely wrong and she reached for the television remote and turned it on. The headline was clear as it scrolled across the bottom of the screen. *Three bank executives dead after boating accident on the Mediterranean.*

To her shock and amazement, the name of the bank scrolled by and her heart raced as she panicked.

"Oh, daddy. I see the news, now. Who was it? What happened?"

"If you were here working you would know. It happened an hour ago and we're just getting the word about it. Why has it been hard to reach you this morning?"

"My phone was off," she said glumly.

"Why would you turn your phone off? It's emergencies like this that I ask you to keep your phone on at all times in case you're needed and right now, you're needed here. Your assistant couldn't reach you either," he said.

"Why didn't you call my personal cell?" she asked.

"Personal cell? You have a personal cell? I didn't remember that."

Reagan felt bad about missing their many calls and texts and her father was deliberately making her feel worse, something he was an expert at. She saw the joys of her wonderful weekend crumbling. She understood that a tragedy happened and she felt horrible about that, but what made her feel worse was that she'd been out of touch with him for four days and he still hadn't asked how she was doing.

"I told Sherry not to bother me or have anyone else bother me. I'm on vacation until Tuesday."

"You were on vacation until Tuesday. I need you back in the office and then packed and making your way to the main office on the west coast. The executives were Mariah Hart, Timothy Foster and Nathan Bridger. I'm handling the press as best I can, but that office is without three of its vice presidents and I need you there. I'm sending Paul Hanks from the Chicago office and Lucas Miller from the Miami office. The three of you need to get control over that office as we deal with the tragedy. You should prepare to stay for several months and maybe even a possible relocation. You have the chance to show what you say you've struggled proving that you've earned. How fast can you get back home?"

"Wait, what? You want me to pretty much move to Los Angeles, just like that? What about the work I'm doing on the expansion in Virginia? You have me overseeing that. The accident just happened and you've already decided who's moving? Don't Lucas and Paul have families? Wives and children? When was it decided who would be going? I thought decisions like that are voted on by all executives and the board," she asked.

Reagan heard the selfish side of her coming out. Her father's request had one meaning for her; she was going to have to leave Keith and the possibility of a relationship with him. Just when she thought her life was taking a turn for the better when it came to her personal life, there was that wrench again.

"If you hadn't shut yourself off from the world to play around New York as if you don't have major responsibilities, you would have been a part of the discussion a few minutes ago when we met and decided. I don't know about Lucas and Paul's personal lives. The call was made and they're going just as you are going."

"Just wait a minute, dad. Don't I get a chance to think about the impact a major move like that will have on me? At least you and I can talk about it and decide what's best."

"Reagan? What is wrong with you? This is not a negotiation. What's best for you is to focus on what's important and that's picking up the pieces of those empty positions in that office, the second largest in the company and keeping the work on track."

"Why is that the only focus? That's far away from you, Jennifer, Renee and mommy. I barely see everyone now and we all live on the same coast. I should have some time to think about this. I understand you wanting me there to smooth things over, but why so long? You're not planning to get new, more permanent leadership in place for that office?"

"I can't go back and forth with you on this. I have a lot to do," he said.

Reagan knew her words were rushed, but she couldn't think clearly. Her father was throwing orders at her too fast for her to digest them logically. She had to move?

"Have you reached out to their families? Are they doing okay?" she asked.

"Whose families?"

Reagan pulled her phone away from her ear and looked at it in wonder at the coldness of her father's tone. His lack of caring surprised her.

"The families of the executives who died. Did you call them and offer the bank's condolences?"

"We have people for that. I'm making sure my Los Angeles office is still standing and operating with leadership in place. There is no way they all should have been on one trip together. That's like a family all flying together on the same plane. What if it goes down?"

Reagan dismissed the chilling sting of his words. For the first time in her life, she saw that his priorities were all screwed up. That's partly why her own life was screwed up.

"I want to talk more about this when I get back home. Can we have lunch or dinner and discuss this move? I have so much I want to tell you about my weekend in New York."

"I will try, but I can't promise I'll have time before you fly out to Los Angeles. I want you there by Sunday evening at the latest. You should be in place and meeting with the staff on Monday morning. Once you've done that, we can set some time up to chat. Do this, Reagan. I know I ask a lot of you, but you're all I have. Your sisters walked away from the legacy, but you stayed around and you're doing a great job. I need another Kelly name in that office. You have to do this and not fight me on the possible move."

"What about my life? What about the plans I have for myself? That doesn't matter? I'm finally trying to take stock in what I want in life and a move could alter that."

"No because you can have a life anywhere. This is the life of an executive; you go where you're needed and right now, that need is in Los Angeles. Enough of this back and forth. Get home as soon as you can and come straight to the office. We're working around the clock for the next few days. The board is meeting tonight at seven and your attendance is not optional; be there."

She started to plead her case more, hoping for the more sensitive side of her father to emerge, but when she heard the click in her ear, she knew he'd hung up.

Her body sagged with disappointment. She'd spent the morning telling Renee of all the ways she was going to change her life and what she looked forward to with Keith and before her new life had a chance to begin, she was thrusts back into her old one; all work, just as Colin had thrown in her face to make fun of her.

Sitting in the chair next to the bed, she was dreading the move to the other side of the country and more than that, she was also going to lose Keith. Her father needed her, pulling at her heart strings as he had a tendency to do. This is what she'd signed up for and it was up to her to help keep the Kelly name associated with the bank. She had to do this. Tears welled up in her eyes. She tried to will the oncoming cry to stay back, but she lost the fight and the flood gates opened. She cried out loud for all that she thought she had gained, but in a split second, watched it all slip right through her fingers. Why did she have to be the one to carry the weight of everyone else's desires? When would she ever get the chance to follow her own?

14

Keith was experiencing the longest elevator ride in his life. Though he and Reagan had agreed to meet for a quick bite to eat before they headed to the airport later, he was too excited about talking to her about solidifying a real relationship. They were about to go their separate ways and he didn't want that.

Having Reagan in his life for four days was in no way going to be enough for him. Unable to wait any longer, he got dressed and decided to surprise her at her room with a proposition. As he rounded the corner to her room, excitement shot through him until he looked down and noticed her packed luggage as if she was leaving. He didn't know what to think when she didn't greet him with her normal smile.

"Hey beautiful! What's going on and what's with the luggage? You're leaving?" he asked.

He knew the response wasn't going to be good when she avoided eye contact.

"Keith. I wasn't expecting you. I thought you would still be asleep."

He opened his mouth to reply and then realized she was planning an escape thinking he would sleep through her exit.

"You were going to leave and not tell me? What's going on, Reagan."

Moving back, he allowed space for her to come out of her room and close the door

"I'm sorry, Keith. I have to leave. I know we were planning to have lunch and everything, but I got a call from my father and there is a major issue. Three of the bank executives who oversee the west coast office were killed in a boating accident and he needs me on the west coast. I have to go home and be ready to leave in a few days."

"I'm sorry to hear that happened. My prayers go up for the families involved. I still don't see how you could just slip out like I wouldn't wonder what happened to you. Not even a goodbye?"

When her shoulders dropped, he knew he was putting her on the spot, but he didn't care. There was more at stake than making her comfortable. She'd lived in that lane for too long.

"I was going to call you when I got to the train station. I'm sorry I have to cut our time short, but this is an emergency and I have to take care of it. My father needs my help," she explained.

"Okay, I understand. Can I see you when you return and have time? I was hoping we could talk about us. What do you think? You won't be on the west coast forever, right?" he asked.

"I don't know if I'll have time. I don't know how long I'll be gone. According to my dad, this may be a semi-permanent move."

"What?"

A few hours ago, she made love to him with tears in her eyes, telling him she had never felt that connected to a man before. When she left to meet Renee at the gym, she was happy and looking forward to not only seeing him later, but also to the discussion about them he told her he wanted to have. In the blink of an eye, that had all gone to hell.

"I'm sorry, Keith. This weekend meant everything to me and under normal circumstances, I would run and jump at the chance at more with you. You have no idea how much I want that, but I can't promise that I will be able to commit to more. I don't know when I'll be back. It's up in the air," she explained.

"So, we are up in the air or we're nowhere?"

He already had his answer before she opened her pretty mouth to speak. She was so beautiful and he couldn't imagine not being able to wake up with her in his arms or make love to her on a lazy Saturday morning. How could she not want the kind of relationship he knew she really wanted and that he wanted with her?

"I don't know when I'll be back. My dad wants me there for a few months to start out and then possibly a lot longer. I knew the plan all along was for me to continue to learn so that I could eventually take over as president one day when he retires. That's been his dream for me since I was a little girl."

"His dream for you? What are your dreams? Do they not matter? You can't have a dream and a man in your life who loves and cares for you and who wouldn't want to see you give up on your dreams? You can't have both me and your career? I have a career too and I would sacrifice every part of it for what I think we can have together. Why do you have to choose?" he asked.

"This is the real Reagan, Keith. I don't know how to have both. I don't know how to have it all. My father needs me to be at the top of my game and that means being in California. I know I'll be back and forth between Maryland and California, but I can't commit to anything else. He's made it clear that he needs me to make my position my priority right now and I have to do that. I enjoyed more in these few days with you than I have in my lifetime. I have never, ever been happier," she said.

"You can have both, but I'm not going to be another person pulling you in the opposite direction. When do you have to leave for that position?" he asked.

"I'm leaving at the end of the week. I'll be in the Baltimore office a countless number of hours this week, preparing for what I'll have to deal with. My father is putting his trust in me that I can do this. It's unexpected and the staff out there is dealing with a major loss. I need to focus on that."

"You're not entitled to a personal life? You told me that other relationships you've had were ruined because the guy didn't respect your desire to be all that you wanted to be, personally and professionally. I know you've only known me for a few days, but you know I'm not like that. I want to see you succeed. I want to be able to celebrate career achievements with and for you. I also want to make love to you every time I can, especially every time you want me to and until we're both seeing stars and our vision is blurry. You say that you believe women can have it all. I guess that means for every woman except you. Faced with the opportunity to have more in your life and you are running away. Do you really want more than the glimpse this weekend provided or have you just been saying you haven't had it because you haven't found the guy who could accept you as you are?"

"Everybody wants something from me and I can't see through it all. It's too much."

"Whoa, what's too much? Me asking you to be in a relationship with me to see where it goes? Your father asking you to choose between what you want for yourself and what he wants for you? Why can't they be one in the same? Does he know about me? About this weekend? About how alive you feel? About how cherished you felt being with me and in my arms? How can you dismiss us so easily? I'm just as shocked as you are that we hit it off so well, but isn't the feelings you've had worth having more of them?"

"No, he doesn't know about you or what my weekend was like. I mean, I tried to tell him, but he only wanted to know that I was making plans to return immediately."

Having enough of the back and forth that wasn't going anywhere, he gave up trying to convince her when her voice cracked from what sounded to him as if she was on the brink of tears.

He moved away from the railing, removed the overnight bag from her shoulder, letting it fall to the floor and took her hand off of the handle of her rollaway suitcase. Needing her close and feeling like she needed to be close to him, he pulled her into his arms and held on tight. He had to let her go, something he knew, and he wasn't going to like it. He needed her to know that if she changed her mind, he would be waiting. He was hoping that once her life settled down, she would miss him enough to want to work out whatever arrangement they could have.

"Baby, listen to me," he whispered close to her ear. He smiled when she exhaled and rested her head on his chest. "I don't want to be another person putting pressure on you to make a decision that you don't want to make for you. I'm not that selfish kind of guy. I want for you whatever it is you want for you. I was hoping you wanted me as much as I want you."

When she sniffled, he knew how hard her choice

was and he didn't want that.

"I'm sorry. I'm so sorry. There is always a hiccup in what I want for myself. It's hard enough having a relationship in the same town, but we'll be on two different coasts. You're about to start production on the movies from your books and that's huge. All of your time will be spent on that and your new book series. You'll be so busy that you won't have time for a woman that far away. I've seen how women look at you. Their eyes were like daggers shooting at me wondering how they can kill me off and take my place on your arm. I saw the looks."

The fact that Reagan was trying to crack a joke let him know that she wasn't shutting herself completely off from him.

"And yet, all I have eyes for is you. That should mean something."

"It does and I'm already jealous at the women who will throw themselves at you. I've seen the ones you've dated. There was a beauty queen, a few A-list actresses and at one time, there was a princess from Milan or someplace like that. Relationships can be ruined by distance. We would be a lost cause. Don't you think it's best to end things now?" she asked.

Keith kissed her on the forehead and decided he was done fighting for something only he wanted. She had to want it for herself or a relationship wouldn't work and he shouldn't have to convince her that they were worth it. He separated from her enough so that he could see her face. When she tried to turn away from his gaze, he pulled her face back to his and he saw them. He saw tears streaming down her face. She wanted him; she wanted them. Her struggle was real. Her wiped her tears and kissed each eyelid softly. He then kissed her cheeks before finally reaching her lips. If he had to say goodbye, he was going to make their last moments together memorable.

"You know how to reach me if you want to or need to. You know where to find me in Baltimore if that's what you want to do. I won't give up on us, but I won't turn into a stalker either," he said, trying to make her smile.

"How did I get so lucky that our paths crossed. I guess this is the part of my life where work takes over any time I would have to think about what I'm losing. I'll have to avoid any press about you, especially if I see you with a new woman or even an old one."

Her attempt to smile fell short. He knew when there was authenticity behind one and he wasn't seeing that.

"Don't go into my past with women I've dated in order to compare them with who you are to me. If I wanted to be with anyone else, I would. I want to be with you, if and when you're ready. You have business to tend to and I want you to do that. I hope you take images of me with you and think about me every single time you roll over in bed and seek my warmth. When you walk around, I want you to still feel your hand in mind. If you desire to see me, I'm a phone call away. I may not be able to run and jump to the west coast, but for the time that you're in Baltimore for the remainder of the week, you know where I'll be. Christmas is in a few weeks and I guess that means you'll be spending it in California. Maybe I can get a phone call or some facetime with you. I'll let you lead and guide what we could be. You already know what I want. How is that?" he asked.

"I'm so sorry I couldn't be better at this," she said.

"Don't you worry your pretty head about this. You do what you need to do. What time is you're your train? You have to leave now?" he asked.

"I do."

"Can I at least go with you to the train station to see you off?"

"I'd like that."

Reaching for her bags, he picked them up, smiled as he linked her arm with his and walked toward the end of what they'd shared. He was still hopeful for a different outcome, but only time would tell if his hope turned out to be fruitful.

15

Fred closed Elijah's bedroom door, finally getting him to sleep after reading him three bedtime stories. He was glad to finally have some quiet time with Renee. She'd been through a busy few days and with the kids both down early, he was looking forward to a late dinner, a glass of wine and his woman in his arms.

"Dinner is almost ready," Renee yelled from the kitchen.

"I told you I have dinner. You were going to take a hot bath while I finished cooking and then we could eat in front of the television, watching something chick-like that you love with a glass of wine in each hand if we wanted to. Why are you at the stove?" he asked, wagging his finger at her.

"Okay, I get the message. I was only adding the pasta to the boiling water. You have the counter full of food you're prepping. What are we having?"

Fred had been home from the office all day working on the movie production schedule with Keith and their team. There was a lot to do and he was already planning a quick trip to Baltimore to meet with the location scouts so that they could begin shooting the trailer for the movie late spring.

"We're having pasta with pesto sauce and grilled shrimp and scallops, your favorite. I'm also making sauteed spinach with mushrooms. We'll kick that off with a Caesar salad and for dessert, I picked up a cheesecake."

"That's sounds delicious. What did the kids eat?"

"They had nuggets and broccoli. I bribed them with ice cream if they agreed to early baths and then bed. They were excited about that," he joked.

"I'm sure. My feet are aching, my back hurts and I can't wait to be off this weekend to do absolutely nothing. Is that on your agenda as well?" Renee asked.

Fred could hear her moving about, no doubt, taking off the shoes that she loved wearing but often complained about. She had already begun taking off her clothes the minute she was in the door.

"It is because next weekend, I'll be in Baltimore. You and the kids should think about joining me. Have you talked to Reagan or your dad?" he asked.

"No. I got a few cryptic texts from Reagan and nothing from my father. I keep getting one of his assistants when I call. The news story about the accident has been all over the news. It's been a few days and it's still the top story of the day. It's terrible and I haven't pushed to connect with Reagan, though I'm mad at her for not calling when she got back to

Baltimore. All I got was a couple of texts saying she was home."

"That's why you should go for a visit. It's been a while since you've been there. It's the Christmas season and you could talk to Reagan about what everyone's plans will be. The final decision of where we'll all be hasn't been decided on yet. Baltimore? Chicago? Here?"

"That's a good idea. She can even bring Keith with her if we have it here or in Chicago. I'm so stoked to know they're all in love and stuff. I was hoping to hear more about it, but I get that things are crazy for her and dad right now."

Fred turned away, not wanting the look on his face to show that her idea of what was going on between Reagan and Keith this week after their weekend together wasn't what she thought it was. He knew he needed to tell her, but he struggled with how to do it without the situation turning bad.

"Do they have a final number of people who died in that accident?" he asked

"Yes. The final count came out this morning It's seven and the only survivor was the wife of one of the bank executives. Last I heard, there hasn't been a cause for the accident. I heard information was still pretty sketchy. At least, that's what I got from the few text messages from Reagan. Wait, I did get one text from my dad that he was handling things."

"Is that all he said to you? Nothing else?"

He'd been thinking of a way to broach the subject of Keith and Reagan for the past two days after his conversation with Keith. It was clear Renee and Reagan had not spoken about it or Renee would be tearing their place up in anger. He did think that she should know what her father did, but he had to be sensitive in his approach. The relationship between Renee and her father wasn't the best, though it was amicable and they communicated when he wasn't too busy.

As he stirred one pot while the seafood sauteed in another pan, he looked up to see Renee enter the kitchen in a t-shirt and nothing else.

"Why, was there something else he should have said? What are you keeping from me? What have you heard?" she asked, sitting at the island.

Fred turned, giving her his full attention. Now was as good a time as any, but he needed to ease his way into it.

"First of all, are you naked under that t-shirt?"

She winked, blew a kiss at him and he had his answer.

"I found it on the sofa and it smelled like you, so I had to put it on. I was going to head to the bedroom and get a shower, but when you asked if that was all my father talked to me about, curiosity got the best of me and here I am. What's up? Should my father have talked to me about something else.?"

Fred turned the fire down under the pasta.

Reagan was keeping her in the dark and that's something he would never do.

"Babe, I'm going to tell you something and I want you to remain calm, okay? I know that's asking a lot because I'm sure you'll want to fly off the handle, but calmness is key here and you don't want to wake the kids," he said.

"Oh, this is something that would have me angry to the point that I could wake my sleeping children? This must be good. Do I need wine first?" she asked.

Instead of answering, he grabbed the bottle and a wine glass and poured her a full glass. It wasn't going to be enough but it was a start.

"I want to go into our history a little before jumping into what I want to say. Be patient, alright?"

"Alright," she answered.

"And calm?" he asked.

"Fred! Stop it. You're scaring me. Is someone hurt? Did someone die? What's going on?"

Seeing her impatience, he came around the counter and sat in the high stool next to her.

"Do you remember what happened when you left your job at the bank and how your father tried to reel you back in but you held your ground because you wanted more out of life than that rat race that was your job?" he asked.

"I do. My father was livid, but he got over it."

"Right. Well, you remember how much pressure your father tried to put on you and the guilt? Oh, the guilt was thick as oil."

"Yeah, but that didn't work on me."

"Right, it didn't work on you, but it worked on Reagan," he said and waited.

"Reagan? What's going on? Did something happen with my father and Reagan?"

"Remember the day Reagan left New York earlier than originally planned?"

"I remember that."

"Remember you promised me calmness. Reagan and Keith aren't together anymore and your dad is sort of in the middle of what happened to them."

Blurting it out was the best way to lay news on Renee; the way someone would rip off a band-aid. He let that live in the air and waited. When Renee looked like she was about to drop her glass to the floor, he quickly reached for it as the shock of his admission hit her.

"What!" she yelled. There was no need in trying to calm her.

"Let me explain."

"You had better and what does this have to do with my father?" she asked angrily.

"He's the cause. He talked to Reagan the morning that she and Keith were leaving New York to head back home, the morning of the boating accident. Your father told Reagan he needed her back in Baltimore to get right to work and then for her to be off to the west coast to oversee the main office there. With today being Friday, I believe she flies out on Sunday."

"What? You know this how?"

"According to Keith, she tried to tell your father about her trip here and she barely got a word in with him. Instead, he went into the accident and how she had a duty and that he wanted her to be one of the people to replace one of the executives who died in the accident. Not that she and Keith were already in a relationship, but she did what equated to breaking up with him because she needed to focus on work and your father needed her to do this. He guilted her into it and since she returned home, she's been avoiding Keith. She told him your father needed her and she didn't think a relationship with Keith would work with her moving and everything."

"I'm going to kill him!"

Fred grabbed her just as she was about to bolt around him, no doubt in search of a phone.

"Renee, you promised me calmness."

"Calmness can go to hell! I will not allow my father to do this to Reagan. Do you know how she has struggled with relationships because of that job? She's never been able to stand up to him, but I can and I will. I promise that I will be as calm as I can, but my father is going to fix this and he's going to do it today."

"You said you've been unable to get beyond his assistants in order to reach him. What do you plan on doing?" he inquired.

"I've been nice and patient, but that's done. They

don't want to mess with me. For work, I can let him ignore me, but when it comes to my sister, I would get in my car, which I hardly ever drive, go straight to his office and demand that he stop bullying Reagan into submission to what he wants. I'm sick of his will hovering over her life."

Fred let her go, knowing nothing he could say or do would change his wife's mind. He silently prayed, not for Reagan or Renee, but for their father. He had no idea what was about to come his way. He stood in the doorway of the kitchen, crossed his legs and arms and watched her pace back and forth in the living room as she dialed.

**

"I don't care where he is or what he's doing. You get my father on this phone right now and tell him it's an emergency!" Renee shouted.

She tried to hold back her anger, but now was not the time to do that. She would deal with her father and do it respectfully, but nicety was not on the agenda. Tapping her foot, she waited and waited and was just about the hang up and dial again when he picked up.

"Renee, darling, what is the emergency and why are you screaming at my assistant? What's wrong?" Ernest asked.

"What did you do to Reagan?" she yelled.

"What? To Reagan?"

"Daddy! What did you do to Reagan? Why is she

practically moving in a few days?"

"Oh, that. I'm putting her in place to run the whole show. Isn't that great? If she can run that, she can show she'll earn her place as president one day. You know, I'm thinking about retiring in a few years and a Kelly will remain at the top."

"I don't give two shakes about the Kelly throne. I care about my sister and you intimidating her to do what you want and not what she wants."

"What do you mean? I have not intimidated her into anything. She wants to do this. She's been working hard to take the helm and this is her big chance. I'm looking out for her career."

Renee's frustration skyrocketed as her anger rose higher and higher at her father's naiveté of what he was really doing.

"Career? That's all you think she cares about? No, dad, that's all you care about. Reagan sees her life in a different direction but because of you, she's back to workaholic Reagan. Do you even know about her weekend here in New York? Have you asked her about it? Before you answer, let me answer for you; no, you don't know. She fell in love last weekend, dad. You heard me – she fell in love and it's with a wonderful man who loves her in return. Do you even care about her personal life or are you only focused on what she can do for you when it comes to work?"

"In love? Who? No way. I think she would have told me something like that and what does that have to do with work? She can be in love and still sit at the top of the family business. Just because you and Jennifer chose..."

"Don't even think about trying to lay your guilt on me. I did what I wanted to do for my life. Did you ask her what she wanted to do or did you just demand she follow your decision for her life? Shame on you for making her feel indebted to you without reason. She wants to stay in Baltimore and enjoy the kind of life we all have, but you refuse to release her to have that. She met a wonderful man, one you actually know and in a few short days, they realized they were meant to be. She walked away from him because she will be in California while he's in Maryland. She's giving up on what she wants and instead is going with what you want. You have to stop doing that to your children. Let us all have our own lives. You can find someone else to send to California and leave Reagan alone. If she wants to go that's different, but don't you want to see her happy? Maybe married with a few children of her own? Don't you want to see her smile more? Don't steal her life from her. You know she loves you and would do anything for you, but not this. Fix this and fix it now. Go talk to her and for once in your life, listen to her. Ask her what she wants and then let her have it or so help me, I will never speak to you again! Do you hear me? I will call Jennifer and together we will never speak to you again. I love you, but I won't let you do to her what you tried to do to me. Fix it now, daddy!"

Before her father could respond, Renee ended the call as she struggled to breathe through her anger. She began to relax when she felt Fred's arms surround her.

"Baby, calm down. You said your peace, now calm down."

"I hurt for her. I have to talk to her. I have to go see her and try to talk her out of leaving."

"Okay, but first, wait and see what your father does. Call Reagan later and if they haven't worked this out, I will drive you straight to Baltimore before the end of the night."

She reached up and held on to Fred's hands.

"She found love and I know her – she didn't put up a fight when my father told her to go. Shame on him."

"I think he heard you and I believe he'll do what you asked and go talk to Reagan. Let's eat, have some wine and take some time to calm yourself. I know you have Reagan's back and she's lucky to have sisters that have her best interest in their hearts," he said.

"Sisters. I need to call Jen and get her in the loop. I bet she'll have a word or two for our father. I promise, one last call and then we'll eat and have a quiet evening."

"Or a road trip with the kids to Baltimore?" Fred asked.

"Yes, or that."

16

"How? How could you have not called him by now? You said you had the most amazing weekend and yet, the man is right here, a few miles down the road and you're acting like he meant nothing to you when clearly that's not the case. You haven't done a bit of work all morning and it's a good thing you took me to your morning meetings to capture action items for you or you wouldn't know what the next few days would look like."

Reagan sulked, pretty much the mood she'd been in since arriving back in Baltimore earlier in the week. True to her father's words, she'd worked around the clock since returning. With more information coming out about the boating accident and what needed to be done, she barely had time to sleep. The highlight of her week stared back at her as she looked around her office. In every empty space and table top in her office, there sat bouquet after bouquet of flowers in a rainbow of colors; all from Keith. Before she arrived at the office on Monday evening after getting off of the train, three beautiful arrangements had been waiting for her. It wasn't until she returned home to her empty house that she realized what was ahead of her; more empty spaces.

"Sherry, enough. I wouldn't know what to say to him," she replied.

"What about what you've said to me, that you're in love with him. I can't believe you're willing to walk away from this man you've been telling me about all week for another office and an empty apartment. Oh, I secured you one of the condo in the building the bank owns. I sent you pictures. Let me know if you want me to change anything or add some color; it's kind of bland, cold and uninviting. You'll be out there alone. Is that what you really want?"

"I caught that and I'll take a look. I asked you to come with me. I can lock in another of the condos in the building for you and the cost would be covered. It would be more money for you and a promotion if you decide to stay permanently."

"You are like the sister I never had, but even with how close we are outside of me being your assistant, I am a woman in love with my man and I want a life with him. Money is not everything when you're building a life with someone. Sometimes you have to make a sacrifice for what you want and my family and friends are here. I believe if something is for me, it's for me and there will be opportunities for me here.

I'm happy and that matters more to me than anything. Moving that far away is too much of a sacrifice for me. It should be for you, too. You've finally found in a man all the things you've been saying you wanted and you walk away from it. Even if you take the job, why give up the man? You can have a long-distance relationship? People do it every day. Sounds to me like you never even gave that a thought."

"You know I have trust issues. Men can stray when out of sight and out of mind."

"Is that how you see him?"

"No, it's not, but what can I do? Besides, I've been ignoring his calls and texts all week because I don't know what to say. All I've done is acknowledged his flowers and cards by saying thank you in a text. I would start typing more and then I delete the words before I hit send. I'm depressing."

"You're in love."

"That too, but what can I do. I can't call Keith now even if I wanted to. I left him with no hope of anything else between us. I think he's tired of reaching out and getting nothing in return."

"Why not? What's stopping you? Pride?" Sherry asked.

Reagan looked up somberly and looked around the room again.

"No flowers today."

"What?" Sherry asked.

"No flowers today. Keith sent flowers Monday,

Tuesday, Wednesday and yesterday, but none today. I think he's given up on me."

"So, you don't want him, but you want him to pretty much beg you for a chance? The man fed your every desire for four days, showered you with flowers and the most beautiful cards in his own words, mind you, and still, you have questions? I can't with you today. You know what, if he has given up on your, I don't blame him. He sent you so many flowers that they are also covering my desk to where I can't greet visitors because I can't see over them. He's thrown out one invitation after the other to go out and you did what you have always done when a man is interested in you – you use work as your excuse. Work is your other boyfriend."

"I wonder if he's missed me at night the way I've been missing him? I miss him so much."

"Then do something about it and don't do this to yourself. You are putting a torch to your own life and for what? It's getting late and I have a few more things to follow-up on before I leave. You sure you don't need me to stay later? You only have two days left here and tomorrow, I'll start packing up your office to send what you want with you in California."

"Go on home. At least one of us has a life outside of here. We can connect tomorrow and let's make it around noon. No need coming in early on a Saturday. I know you could use a break and your man has probably missed you this week."

"Reagan?"

"Yes?"

"Your man is missing you too. Look around this office and you'll see his heart in every petal and his love in every word of the ten or so cards he sent you this week and it's only been four days, just like the number of days it took for you to fall in love with him. It's not a coincidence. Holler if you need anything. I'll tidy up and head out."

When Sherry left, Reagan took out her cell phone, turned to watch the snow falling outside the window and pulled up the pictures she had from her weekend. She scrolled through one picture after the other and found herself on the verge of tears over what she allowed to slip through her fingers. Keith's handsome face smiled back at her and her heart wept.

"Reagan?"

Jostled out her nostalgic, she turned around to her father standing on the other side of her desk.

"Hi, daddy. Am I late for a meeting or something? I lost track of time," she said.

"No, nothing like that. I came to talk to you, baby girl. Got a minute?" he asked.

Reagan was all out of sorts. She had to have done something wrong or messed something up or maybe missed a call or meeting that was important to him. She couldn't seem to think straight. It wasn't often her father stopped by her office without a scheduled appointment.

"You're sure nothing is wrong?" she asked.

He sat and she found herself making sure she was sitting up straight and looking for a pen to take notes of whatever he was dropping by to discuss; it had to be work related.

"I lied," he uttered softly. "There is something wrong. What I've done to you is wrong."

"I don't understand. What have you done to me?" she asked.

"Let me see if I can explain this to you from the beginning. When I met your mother, I was crazy in love with her. I mean, I would do anything for her and that's why I worked so hard to take over the bank when my father died. I wanted to be able to provide your mother with anything she wanted to make her happy. I worked day and night to get us here and there have been good and bad times along the way. The good were your mother and you three girls. You were why I worked so hard, but on the bad side, I never spent as much time with the four of you like I should have. I missed holidays, birthdays, school events and dances. I wasn't around when any of you said your first words or took your first steps. When you won your first gymnastics championship, I was in Paris on business. I was late for Renee's high school graduation and didn't hear when her name was called. I know your mother did a lot of apologizing for my absences, but I told myself it was okay because as a husband and father, I was doing my job of providing for my family. There were many other times when I missed important things in our lives and I made myself feel better about that by reminding myself that what I was doing, I was doing for you all. I wasn't. I did it because I wanted to succeed and I knew your mother was there to take care of you and your sisters."

"Daddy, we understood."

"I know and I love you girls for that, but that didn't make my absence in your lives as you were growing up palpable excuses. I know that I put a lot of pressure on you, Renee and Jennifer to step up to the plate and be able to take over my position one day and that was wrong. Those two fought me tooth and nail so that they could carve out the lives they wanted for themselves and not the ones I wanted for them. You? You are different than them. It's not that you don't have the strong will to fight for what you want, but you have always been the one to want to make me happy despite what it would do for your own happiness. Until now, I didn't pay attention to what I have done to you. I had Sherry pull up your schedule for the past few months and I couldn't believe the long hours you spend doing the bank's business. What time are you carving out for the things you want in life? I know you have the new house and you bought a new car, but what else is there that you want that you don't have? That's not a question for you as much as it is a question for me. I already know and his name is Keith Jackson."

Reagan gripped the edge of her desk tight the moment her father said his name. He knew. How could he? And then she knew; Renee.

"Renee called you, didn't she? She had no right to do that."

"Don't be mad at her. She read me the riot and I mean she let me have it. She did it with the utmost respect, but yeah, she laid it on me that I put too much pressure on you to be like me. I lost your mother because I was being me and I didn't pay my wife the attention she needed. So much so that she's getting married to a man who has given her what she begged me for throughout our marriage. She wanted time with me and I couldn't see that I could lose her because I never put her first. Renee was right when she said that it was up to me to release you from the tight grip I have had you in since you joined the leadership team. For that, I am sorry."

"Don't apologize, daddy. I love my job. Really I do."

"But do you love it enough to walk away from Keith? He's a great guy, sweetheart. I've known that since the moment I met him when your sister asked me to work with him years ago when he started making big bucks from his book sales and had an interest in investments. I hear the two of you really hit it off and I assume he's the reason behind all the flowers that keep appearing around here?"

"He is and I love them."

"Do you love him too? I'm talking about Keith?"

"It was a weekend, daddy."

"Reagan, stop. Don't do that. This is me you're talking to. I asked you a question. Don't try and deflect. I asked if you love him. Do you?" Ernest asked again.

"I do. I fell in love with him in a matter of hours, daddy. Who does that? How is that possible? It was a few hours and before you compare it to what Renee experienced with Fred, I know about that."

"That happened with you and Keith, just in a different way. Now what? Do you choose work over your heart? Let me just say that I wish I could go back and make better choices and maybe I wouldn't be divorced from the world's greatest woman."

"You're counting on me."

"Reagan, stop it. This isn't about me; it's about you and Keith. I can see it in your eyes that you want to choose your heart, don't you?"

"More than anything. I think about him all the time. I miss hearing his voice and laughing at his corny jokes and he has a lot of them. I miss him, daddy."

"See, this is not what I never wanted for any of you. I didn't want your mother to feel like being married to me was a death sentence and I don't want my daughters sacrificing their happiness for the sake of a job. When your sisters called me an hour ago, and yes, both called to tell me to back off, I didn't realize I was being a tyrant. You should choose love. Life is too short not to."

"Are you saying I have to give up my job in order to have a life with Keith if I want one?" she asked.

"No, not at all. You can have both. You don't have to sacrifice what you feel for him for what you want around here. Effective this week, I'm making some changes because you're not the only one I've kept my thumb on. I have to do better and that begins today."

"Are you firing me?"

"No. Listen and stop interrupting and raising your own blood pressure. If you don't want to go to Los Angeles, then don't go, and I mean that. Someone else will, undoubtedly, step up. I won't be upset if you choose love. I run the bank with an iron fist and I think more about the business than the families that make up the business. You asked me if I had reached out to the families of those who died and remember how callous my response was and I don't want to be that uncaring. I had my assistant, Heather, check into people's vacation time for the past two years and I discovered, most people never take theirs. They feel obligated to work even when they haven't had time off in months. That's not the kind of company I want. I want an equal balance of work and home life. I've been walking around the building, floor after floor watching people give everything they have, even staying well after midnight this week and still showing up before six in the morning. That's dedication. I love it and respect it, but I don't want that to be the priority anymore. I've seen what I've done to you and I don't like it. You have that same kind of dedication, even the kind that you're willing to forgo love with a great man, one I know personally who I would love to see with my youngest daughter on his arm."

"Thank you, daddy."

"I'm going to increase the staff at the office here and at the satellite offices. I'm going to add on two additional vice presidents for each position we currently have. In other words, there will be three vice presidents over operations and expansion here in Baltimore and you will work together to make sure work life and home life are balanced better. You need help and so do the other officers. We have the money to cover the new staff and so I'm doing that with the full support of the board. I'm also adding a lot more administrative staff to help make sure you get things done and can get out of the office at a decent hour to have a life whether you stay here or leave; that goes for everyone. I made sacrifices that I don't want to see you make. I'm working with my team to figure out how to implement this, but for now, the few changes I can make without board approval, I will do."

"You've really been thinking about this and just within the past hour or so? Go daddy!" Reagan applauded.

"I'm learning. Now, it's Friday and starting today, I'm giving everyone tomorrow off and all-day Monday as well. I don't want to see or hear of anyone coming into the building to get any work done until at least Tuesday morning. Once a month, we're going to have a Friday where everyone is going to be off with pay to enjoy time with family or just to have time to exhale. Our days are hectic and still, there is a lot of work that gets done to keep us running and I want to show my appreciation. There are people in the west coast office who can keep that place running like a well-oiled machine and I'm going to put my faith in them to do that. I'm going to fly out there next week to check on everything, but you? I want you to think long and hard and realize what you want and not what I want. What I want most of all is for you to have a life filled with love and fun and a good man; Keith is that. I want you to get out of here and go find your young man. I heard he lives right here in Baltimore. I saw a news story a month ago about his big move to this area and what he and Fred are working on. Don't you dare sacrifice the love you have found. It may not come around again and who knows, I may get another son-in-law and some more grandchildren out of this," Ernest joked.

"Daddy!"

Reagan was embarrassed. She and her father never talked about anything personal, something she just realized. They were always about business. This was new and she liked it.

"Don't daddy me. Your sisters threatened me and

so did your mother. After I talked to them, she called me and gave me a piece of her mind too. I guess today was the day to get me straight. They were fine with me meddling in their lives, but they came with guns drawn when it came to you. I'm going to let you finish up here, but then I expect you to get out of here. I've already gave instructions to have everyone who is still here notified that they should shut it down and head out."

When he stood, Reagan stood with him and came around her desk, hugging him tight.

"I love you, daddy. Are you taking tomorrow off too?"

"I sure am."

"What are you going to do with your time off until Tuesday?" she asked.

"I'm going to take the train to New York to visit with my grandchildren who only know me via phone chat. Next month, right after the new year, I'm heading to Chicago to visit Jennifer and her family. I'm hoping that we can all have a nice Christmas together this year at my house. I want to do it up big with decorations and food – lots of food. I'm going to ask Renee about that this weekend, since I feel like I need to repair things with her in person. What do you think about that? You can bring Keith and we can sit around with the grandkids and watch movies, eat pizza and do other fun things. I've missed out on too much time with you all and I don't want to miss any more. I'm thinking of inviting your mother and her fiancé. I hold no grudges and I want to be sure we're all still a family."

"Renee told me over the weekend about mom's engagement."

"Yeah, I know. Your mother actually called and told me herself. I'm happy for her. I won't lie and say it doesn't hurt because it does. I still love her very much, but I understand."

"I'm sorry you're in pain."

"I never want you to feel the pain I feel in losing your mother. Before I leave and before you run out of here to maybe talk to Keith, tell me about your weekend with him. What did you do? What did you see and most of all, what did you eat? They have the best food in New York!"

"Do you have some extra time tonight?" she asked.

Though she was ready to run out and find Keith, what she wanted most of all was uninterrupted time with her father.

"I have all the time in the world for you."

"Good. Can we have dinner?" she asked.

"Of course. We haven't done that in ages; just me and you. Where do you want to go?" Ernest asked.

"Right here. Let's order some subs and pizza and maybe even some wings and just talk. I have so much I want to tell you about New York and some other stuff."

"I've missed your life, haven't I?" he asked.

She saw self-disappointment on his face and she didn't want that. After the pandemic of over a year ago, she didn't want to focus on what happened in the past; she wanted to focus on the now and the future.

"You won't miss anymore and I'm going to see to that. I still want to make you proud of me and I promise, I will. I know when mom was pregnant with me, you wanted me to be the son you didn't have."

When her father took both of her hands in his, she held his gaze.

"You won't remember this but, when your mother was pregnant with you, we each chose a boy name and a girl name for you. Yes, I wanted a son, like most men do, but more than that, I wanted a happy healthy baby. You came into this world screaming at the top of your lungs. When they finally handed you to her, you wouldn't stop crying. She tried to soothe you and I stood on the side smiling while she worked on bonding with you. She started saying, *'Alisa, it's okay – mommy is here'*. That was the name she originally picked for you. She said that name over and over again, but you wouldn't stop crying. I walked over, took you out of her arms and whispered, *'Reagan, stop giving your mommy all this fuss and calm down so that she can feed you.'* That was the name I picked for you. In an instant, you quieted, held my finger tight in your hand and you looked right at me. The crying had stopped. When the nurse asked what your name would be because she heard us call you two different names, your mother shouted 'REAGAN'. She said since you didn't answer to her name for you, yet you answered to Reagan, she knew that in the future, it was that name that would quiet you down. At that moment, I didn't think of or continue to dream of a son. I loved you just as I loved and still love, your sisters who were at home waiting for us to bring you to them. We were happy, there was a lot of love and I never once loved you any less because you were not a son. You make me proud daily and if, like your sisters, you find some other career, I will support that and love you."

"Daddy, I don't want to leave the bank. I love everything about it, except for not being able to see the forest for the trees. Keith is there in my forest and I want him and the trees. I want me and you to have more father/daughter time and more time with me, Jen and Renee. We all want that. Now, for that pizza because I'm starving."

"What about Keith?" Ernest asked.

"If he still wants me today, I think he will tomorrow too. Tonight, I have a lot that I want to share with you and who knows when I'll have you all to myself without interruption. Sherry?" she yelled into the outer office.

When she showed up in the doorway in a heartbeat, there was no doubt Sherry had been listening.

"Menus, right?" she asked.

"Yes. Give me every one you have and then you head out. I'll be fine. I'll see you Tuesday."

"Tuesday?" Sherry asked.

"You're on paid vacation until Tuesday. Reagan's not moving, so she won't need help packing and I'll see that she gets home safe. Thanks for all you do for the bank," Ernest said.

Reagan couldn't be prouder than she was at the moment. Her elation would extend into the next day when she got up and went in search of her man.

17

Keith sat in front of the large screen television as a movie played, which he had no idea what it was. For the past hour since he last moved, it had been watching him instead of him watching it. Before him were the edits to his latest novel and unlike any other time when he received them from his editor, he couldn't focus on the storyline enough to dive into the updates and decide on those he wanted to keep and those he wanted to ignore. Nothing could take his mind off of Reagan and wondered if she struggled with missing him as much as he was missing her.

Throwing the papers to the seat next to him, he picked up the remote and flipped through several channels, no station actually capturing his attention. He was too frustrated that he could no longer have Reagan in his arms. He longed for the ability to turn back the hands of time and go back to that Saturday night when they shared, not only their bodies, but their minds and their spirits.

How much longer was he planning to wait before showing her that he'd fallen in love with her? He'd only been in love once and that love had taken a year to blossom. As special as Reagan was to him, he had no doubt that his love for her was genuine. What was she feeling? Was it just good sex for her that weekend and now she wanted to go back to her normal routine?

"Forget this," he said out loud.

He knew what he was going to do. He was going to let her know that he would be here waiting for her and willing to fly to see her every week for a day or two if that was what they needed to keep their connection and love alive. She was worth it; what they had was worth it.

His ringing phone broke into his thoughts. He saw Carl's number and started to send him to voicemail, but he knew that would only cause Carl to keep calling until he reached him.

"Carl, I can't have this conversation with you right now; I have some place to be."

"Where?" Carl asked.

"Why do you need that much information? Look, I understand the pressure you're under and I appreciate you as my agent and my friend and that you're looking out for me, but I have someplace important to go."

Grabbing his keys, he headed for the door.

"Keith, work with me here."

"I will as soon as I get back and I promise, once I get a situation worked out and know where I stand once and for all, I'll get my mind back in the game. It's not there at this moment."

"How long will you need?" Carl asked.

"I'll call you in a few hours. How's that? I'm throwing you a bone here and you know it. Buy me a little time and I'll check back in and give you my full attention. Something else needs my attention right now and I know you can understand that. I love all this work and money making, but it's not what's most important. I know that and I don't think I've ever known that before. It's like a lightbulb went off in my life recently and I can't turn it off until I reset my life. I need time to do that."

"Wait? Is this about Reagan Kelly? You told me about her earlier this week. What's up, man?"

"The one and only. I need to see her and it can't wait."

"Why didn't you tell me this was about Reagan? This is Ernest Kelly's daughter, right?" Carl asked.

"Yes, and I need to make some things right with her or I'm never going to be able to get my focus back on track."

Keith stepped out of the elevator and rushed toward through the lobby to get to his car parked less than a block away.

"I'm with you. Call when you're through and good luck. The love of that woman is more important than anything. I remember hearing the love you have for her in your voice when you told me more about her. She sounds amazing and I can't wait to meet her. I know things are going to work out fine."

"I sure hope so."

Before he could get much further, to his surprise, Reagan was walking toward him. Was she real or had he been thinking about her so much that he was now seeing her in his mind and visualizing her presence before him?

He almost dropped his phone when he heard the sweet sound of her voice saying his name. Was he dreaming?

Disconnecting the call with Carl without even telling him the call was over, he walked straight for her.

"You're here!" he yelled and didn't care that he had practically shouted.

"Yes I am. You're leaving?" she asked.

"Baby! You're here in my building."

He wanted to say more, but he couldn't. He was too happy to see her. Taking her by the hand, he moved them to a more private part of the lobby. He would head for the elevator, taking her up to his place and never letting her leave him again, but he waited.

Reaching for her, he picked her up off of her feet and into his arms. After thinking and dreaming about having her in his arms again, he wasn't about to lose the opportunity to really test that she was actually with him.

"Yes, I was coming to see you," she said.

"Kiss. Lips. First."

That's all he could get out. The last thing he wanted to do was talk; he needed to feel. The kiss was life to him. He felt a renewed sense of being as the kiss turned wild and ravenous. He tried and still could not get enough of her. If it wasn't for a few people clearing their throats around them, he didn't know if he'd let her lips free.

"Hi to you too!" she said.

"I can't believe you're here. I was on my way to your building. I couldn't take being away from you for another day. I was on my way to beg you to give us a try, but now you're here!" he beamed.

"Yes, I am and I'm sorry for doing that to you. I loved all the flowers and cards you sent me. I'm sorry I was being pigheaded by not calling you."

"Baby, you're here now and that matters. Wait, are you here for a good or a bad reason? You here to tell me to stop bugging you with flowers?"

"No, of course not. I loved all of them. My office is covered in flower vases and people keep stopping by to see what you sent that was new and then they stopped and I couldn't breathe thinking that I'd waited too long or that I'd been playing a dangerous game with your heart. I never meant to do that. I was being stupid based on past practices and that was wrong."

"I love you, Reagan. I know it sounds crazy, but it's true – I love you. I know we agreed to have that weekend, but it wasn't enough for me. I'm dreaming of so much more for us."

"I love you too and that's what I was coming here to tell you."

"Really? You love me, too?" he asked jubilantly and pulled her even closer in to his embrace.

"If you'll have me, I promise to never do that again. I want to be with you and share everything and every part of my life with you."

"Even with you living on another coast? You're still willing to try because I definitely want to?"

"What?" he questioned when she smiled and was pretty much bouncing around in place. He didn't know what was the cause.

"I'm not moving. I'm going for about a week and that's because I want to check in on the staff and see what I can do to help, but I'm coming back to my position here."

"Really? You're not playing with me, are you?"

"Well, I actually came here to play with you tonight if you're free."

He heard it. There was that sexy undertone that had him picking her up in his arms and racing back to the elevator before she changed her mind.

"I'm free for as long as you need and want me to be. We have a lot of planning to do, especially a nice island trip for New Year's Eve. I'm thinking Maldives? You game?"

"You've been thinking about this already?"

"Baby, I've been planning trips in my head since the moment you told me of all the places you wanted to go. As long as we're together, we are going everywhere! First, we're going up to my place, I'm going to strip you naked and I'm hoping you don't have plans for tomorrow. You have some making up to do for how you've tortured me this week being without you."

"As soon as I'm back in the office next week, I'm going to put in for some vacation time for that trip. I'm already excited and I can't wait to go shopping for more sexy bathing suits. I can't even find the white one I wore when we went swimming."

Keith chuckled. He would wait to tell her that he kept it. She must have forgotten that she changed out of it when they went back to his suite and when she left the next morning, she forgot to take it down where it was left drying in the bathroom.

"Make sure I'm with you so that I can be your personal bathing suit checker. I have a good eye, only for you!"

"You're on and you in speedos? I'm ready to go now!" she joked.

"I love you, Reagan."

"I love you, too. I almost forgot - I actually have all weekend off. My dad closed the offices down and he's heading to New York to see my sister. I'm all yours and ready for another unforgettable weekend. How's that for the start of me making it up to you?"

Keith didn't respond. In the elevator alone with her, he wrapped her legs around his body, held her up and prayed that the elevator up the few floors would take a lifetime. He needed the kiss to last that long.

Epilogue
3 Years Later

Reagan tried her best to sit comfortably on the large gray sofa in the local television studio as she waited for Keith's interview to begin. There was a slight delay as the producer worked to make sure they had Fred on at the same time since he would be doing the interview with Keith, but from a studio in New York City. This was her husband's big day and being a little or even a lot uncomfortable didn't matter to her. He'd worked hard to finally see his dream of making movies come to life. She had been nervous that she would be late after a meeting at the bank ran late. When Keith told her that they wouldn't begin the interview until she arrived since it was being taped to play later in the week, she told him why she was running a little late and he told her that what she was about to do was well worth the wait.

After getting back together that day three years ago

in his condo after making the decision to not move to California, they spent the rest of the weekend in bed, reacquainting themselves. Over the next several weeks, she showed him around Baltimore, even sights she didn't know existed. The highlight of the end of the year was spending Christmas with her family at her father's house and then spending New Year's Eve and the following week on a private island, just the two of them. Since that time, traveling had become one of their favorite things to do when they had down time, which she happily made room for in her busy work life. This year for Christmas, the entire family was spending it with her and Keith as they waited the birth of twins in a few months.

"Daddy, daddy!"

Reagan turned and tried to get up and grab her son, Keith Jr., who they called, KJ, before he darted onto the stage as the cameras were about to roll. Unable to move as fast as she usually could before being six months pregnant, she gave her mother, Sarah, a side look as she bounded around a corner in an attempt to grab the eighteen-month-old, but she didn't quite make it. As the interview was about to begin, KJ saw Keith and beelined straight for him, not caring that they were about to record.

"Whoa," Keith said as KJ ran straight for his outstretched arms. "I got you. Daddy got you," he said soothing KJ just before he burst into tears.

"I'm sorry," her mother said walking over to her.

"He wanted to get down just as I reached the door and he heard his father's voice. You know how he is about Keith."

"I know mom and it's okay. Look, he's sitting still," Reagan said, happy that she didn't have to make another attempt to get up. The twins were weighing her down.

"Maybe I should go get him. This is an important interview for Keith. There is already talk that this first movie is going to be the biggest box office of next year. Early projections have it mirroring the numbers from when the first Black Panther movie was released years ago. Imagine that," Sarah exclaimed. "It's going to be big!" she added. "I heard they're doing this recording locally, but it's actually for a national news show."

"It is. He didn't want to travel with me being pregnant. With twins, you never know when they'll make an entrance and he wanted to stay close.

"He spoils you like crazy!" Sarah chimed.

"I know," Reagan tried to whisper to not be heard.

"I thought you were going to be at work. Does Keith know you're over here?"

"He saw me and waved. He was already on the set when I walked in. I sat here in the corner and waited. I was at work at a meeting, that wasn't actually my meeting, but I wanted to be on it to gloat. I didn't know you had KJ."

"Oh, I didn't. He's been with Keith all day. I offered to come and help so that KJ could get his nap in while you were at the bank working today. I asked if he wanted me to call you and he said no, that you were getting off early anyway and he was planning to go home right after the interview wrapped up. Why were you gloating at work?"

Reagan smiled to herself. She thought of how petty she had been earlier and could have been worse at it, but she pulled back a little.

"Do you remember Colin Evers? I dated him back in college?" she asked.

"I sure do and I never liked him."

"No one did, yet no one told me back then."

"What does he have to do with anything?"

"He did a video conference call interview for the job of running one of our new satellite offices, the one in Houston, Texas. I know it was petty, but I wanted him to see me. I didn't owe him anything, but he had this image of me and I wanted my belly to dispel that."

"Ah, I see. What happened?"

"I walked into the room just as the interview started and you should have seen the look on his face. After it was over, he asked to speak to me privately. Everyone walked out and I remained in the room, looking at him on the screen. He wanted to apologize for how he's treated me in the past and said he'd heard that I was overseeing all of the senior staff of the bank offices, nationwide. What he didn't know was that I was married, had KJ and was pregnant with twins. Daddy mentioned it to him before the interview began. I asked about his wife and children and he said he was divorced, twice now and was learning what he had to offer a woman material wise didn't make up for what she wanted from him emotionally and mentally. He apologized profusely. I asked him if he was apologizing because he thought that I would have a hand in whether he got the job or not. He said he understood if I persuaded my father to not hire him. I wanted to be even pettier at that moment, but I didn't. I have the life I've always wanted and there was no reason to see him grovel, though I wanted to. I wanted him to see me having a personal life and still at the top of my game in the office. He never thought I was capable of both. I ran into him once a few years ago and he was horrible to me. No need to hold onto that grudge especially with how blessed my life is. I have a job I love, my family and a husband who loves me and treats me as if we fall in love again and again every single day; and we do."

"What did you say to your father?"

"He asked me what my thoughts were because the branch Colin would oversee would have him reporting to me. Everyone deserves a chance. Look at the major change in Buster, who you know I hated. He found a woman who wouldn't put up with his mess and he knew he had to change in order to not lose her. Colin has redemption ability and I would never stand in his way. Daddy is going to hire him. He'll only have to deal with me for a few more months and then I'm not returning to work until the twins are five. I want time with all of them while they're still young."

"Good for you. That time is precious. What are your plans for the day? I want to help you decorate for Christmas. Are Keith's sisters still coming to town for in two weeks?"

"Yes, and Erika is coming back when the twins are born. Today, I'm planning to take KJ to the playground to let him run around. He loves that place."

"Amazing," Sarah said.

"What?"

"That you and Keith are able to manage huge careers and make plenty of time for family and making more babies," she laughed.

"We promised each other that the weekend that we met would not be the only unforgettable time of our lives. We promised to make memories that were unforgettable each and every day and that starts with making sure we had plenty of family time. We have money, wealth and are living our dream life and we want to make sure KJ and this one that I'm carrying know that we will be a constant presence in their lives."

"No issues about not being bank president? I know you were working toward that a few years ago."

"I was doing that for daddy and the company. I'm living my life for me and senior vice president is good enough for me. Maybe one day that will change, but not before my kids are all grown. I want to have more babies after these two and I want to be a mommy that my children know. I have what I want out of my career and most of all, I have the perfect life with the most unforgettable man on earth."

"Yeah, that husband of yours is pretty incredible and look at KJ, already falling asleep in his lap. All he wanted was to be with his daddy. More babies, huh?"

Reagan rubbed her growing belly.

"Yep, and Keith's talking about maybe two more; I think one more will be plenty. We're trying to keep up with Renee. Did I tell you that the weekend I met Keith, Renee was pregnant with Kayla, baby number three and didn't know it? Now they have four with Stevie being two months old. I should have known with the number of times she kept running to the bathroom during the concert that weekend. How long are you staying in town this time or are you here just for the Christmas holiday?"

"Your father wants to stay until after you have the babies."

"Speaking of daddy, where is he anyway? I thought he left the bank before I did?"

"He's playing golf. I wanted to see you and KJ and I told him to go meet up with his friend. It's not usually this warm in Baltimore in December and he wanted to take advantage of that. We're playing cards with some friends later this evening."

"I can't believe you and daddy remarried after

being divorced for all those years. Are you going to ever tell me how it happened? How did you end up with daddy when you were set to marry another man; Walter, I think?"

"Well, it was like this. Your father and I ended up in New York visiting Renee at the same time over that weekend when you got back together with Keith, the week after you met. After I got there, Renee bailed on me with plans we made to see a play and I decided to still go and when I got there, your father was in the other seat that had been Fred's. At first, I was going to leave, but he invited me to stay and enjoy the show with him. I did and then we went to dinner at this little out of the way diner where we sat talking and eating cherry pie all night. We really talked that night and for the first time in years, sitting and having a conversation with him wasn't interrupted by bank business. That was some coincidence, huh?"

Reagan didn't say anything. She had a feeling it wasn't a coincidence at all; something she herself could attest to. What she knew was that her parents had gone out on a date for Valentine's day a few years back and months later, they were remarried in a private ceremony, only telling her and her sisters after they were back. They had kept their budding romance a secret, telling Renee that her setup didn't work when it actually had.

"I guess you could say you had one of those unforgettable kind of weekends?" Reagan asked.

"Yeah, I guess you could say that. I guess you and I both had unforgettable weekends in New York."

"Things are good with you and daddy?"

"I won't say better the second time around because the first time wasn't all bad. This time though, he is all over me and I love it. Everything about your father and I being back together has been unforgettable, just like what you still share with Keith."

Reagan leaned back as the interviewer began with introducing Keith and Fred.

"Unforgettable, indeed."

Get this new release from Cheryl Barton, available today!

Baby, Come Back

Meridian, Mississippi, held nothing but bad memories for Sumaria Moore. Not only did she lose her parents who raised her in the southern town, but the love of her life had walked out on her three years ago, leaving not only their love behind, but a secret he never knew about.

Preston Washington wanted more than what a small, southern town could offer him. In order to make his dreams come true, he had to leave the only life he knew behind.

A bad decision took them away from each other and a tragedy brought them once again to the town neither wanted to go back to. Sumaria and Preston will soon find that the best kept secrets aren't the ones that are kept hidden; they are the ones that can show them how everything they left behind, could lead them to what they thought they once had; forever.

Here is a quick look into an upcoming release, *Seize the Moment* – a story about rekindling love during a world-wide, COVID-19 pandemic.

"You're a stupid fool!"

Aubree looked away from her best friend, Penelope, crossed her legs as she sat on the end of the desk and nervously tapped her one foot on the carpet.

"I'm no fool," she replied.

"Oh, yes you are. Who ends a relationship in the middle of a pandemic? Girl! There is a virus going around, a very dangerous one and you're mad because he didn't have the Valentine's Day planned out that you wanted? Like you couldn't plan something. Ugh, women like you piss me off! Your whole life pisses me off!"

Penelope, looking at the back of Aubree's head picked up a paperclip and through it at her in an attempt to get her to turn around and face the music.

"Hey!" Aubree yelled and moved from the desk to the chair in front of Penelope's desk.

"Oh, be quiet. It was a paperclip. I thought about tossing the stapler at you, but if I had really hurt you, I could be fired," she joked.

"Please," Aubree said and sucked her teeth. "I'm your best friend and your boss and I wouldn't fire you. Like you said, we're in the middle of a pandemic and after today, who knows when we'll be able to see each other in person again. I can't fire my best friend and expect her to still be my best friend."

"Yet, again, you can ruin a relationship with a man who is every woman's wet and dry dream – the very fine and extremely handsome, debonair and hot as fire Russell Hall! Let me repeat myself – you are a stupid fool!"

"What was I supposed to do? He doesn't listen to me when I say pay more attention to me."

Penelope got up and walked around to sit in the other chair in front of her desk. She and Aubree had been having this conversation for the past month, ever since she decided that she would try and teach her boyfriend a lesson by breaking up with him in hopes that he would get on bended knee and beg her to not leave him. She played with fire and got burned.

"You were supposed to understand that he works hard just like you do. You and Russell are workaholics and I do remember you sending me out on a run to pick up gifts for your man. How *suck'ish* like is that? Huh?"

When Aubree pouted and folded her arms across her chest, Penelope laughed at her.

"At least I got him something. He didn't get me anything until a day later."

"No – that's a lie. If you're going to talk bad about him, tell it right. You said you faked being asleep when he got in that night because you were mad. If you weren't acting like a child, you would have gotten your gift and a little bit more, but no, you had to go to the extreme and now look at you."

"He didn't even come home last night," Aubree whined.

"Now you're checking when he comes and goes? You're not together anymore! Hello! Remember that?"

"We still live in the same house, for now, and the least he could do is be respectful and not stay out all night. He was probably with some woman. Why else does a man stay out all night if not to get something on the side."

"It's not on the side anymore – *YOU BROKE UP WITH HIM*!" Penelope shouted and when a few heads in the outer office looked their way, she got up and slammed her office door to shut them out.

"So dramatic and unnecessary, slamming the door in their faces like that!" Aubree said pointedly.

"I know you're not talking about me be dramatic and doing unnecessary things. Those are your double middle names – Miss Dramatic and Miss Unnecessary."

"Stop berating me and help me. I think Russell has found a place to live."

"Why do you care? Isn't he letting you stay in the house that he's paying the mortgage on? I know you make good money and could afford that big beautiful house, but still, girl, you had a man taking good, good care of you and you get mad because of what? This is a man who would have you stumbling in here on wobbly legs with your kitty cat deliciously sore from what he laid on you before you came in the office and you broke up with him for what? I can't stand you. If we weren't best friends, I'd hit on him."

When Aubree tried to hit her on the arm, Penelope jumped out of her chair and stood by the office door.

"Don't even joke like that or I'd have to cut you."

"Whatever. What's the problem? You broke up with him and he's moving out at your request. What is your problem today? What can sister Penelope help you out with today to fix your little miserable life?"

There was a long pause and Penelope thought Aubree wasn't going to answer. When she looked over, Aubree's head was done and the words she spoke were soft, almost at a whisper and were directed at the floor.

"Make him stay."

Usually at this time, Penelope would have a quip to throw back at her as part of their usual banter, but when she looked at Aubree's downturned face, she saw something she'd never seen before; she saw a serious plea.

"Wait, we're not exchanging our usual tit-for-tat anymore, are we? You're serious? Since when? Is it because he stayed out all night and you think he was with another woman or is it because we're all about to be under a stay-at-home order and you don't want to be alone?"

"Neither. It's because I love Russell and I think he's finally tired of all the games I play. I don't know what's wrong with me. I can't do anything right. I can't keep him or break up with him right. What can I do? He may move out with this stupid pandemic so that he doesn't have to get stuck with me for who knows how long. Help me!" Aubree pleaded.

Penelope thought for a moment and then sat back in the chair and turned it around so that they were facing each other.

"Okay, this is what you do and do not mess this up. This COVID-19 pandemic is a terrible thing, but you can actually seize the moment and show Russell that you didn't mean to make a hasty decision to end things. You'll only get one chance at this, so make it count."

"I'm ready. What do you have in mind? This better be good."

"Girl, when this works for you, I'm going to bottle this idea up and sell it so that I can quit this job and no longer have to slave away for my tyrant boss! Now, listen up."

Get your copy of "Seize the Moment"
in March 15, 2021
Preorder your copy today at
www.cherylbarton.net

His Holiday Wife
A Short Love Story

Maia Dutton found herself working three jobs while also finishing up her doctorate degree. She's been struggling for years to come up with the money to pay for the ultimate two-week graduation trip to New Zealand, Tahiti and Bora Bora. One day, an opportunity fell at her feet, or in reality, she fell at the feet of an opportunity and for a month, all she had to do was pretend to be the wife of a man who could pay for her trip a million times over.

Baron Colter has put his mother off for the last time and now she was coming to collect or he would never get the chance to run her multi-million-dollar fashion dynasty. He had one last opportunity to live up to her rule for having the company turned over to him or she would never retire. What he didn't expect was to have the fate of his future placed in the hands of a woman with two left feet who doesn't know the difference between a salad fork and a dinner fork.

Baron finds Maia interesting and entertaining and before thirty days are up, he's going to find it hard to live without her.

Get your copy of "His Holiday Wife" late 2021
www.cherylbarton.net

"The Brothers of Chi-Town", I Can't Let Go – now available for download and in paperback.

Carter Garrison vowed to love, honor and cherish his wife, Sienna, forsaking all others, something he forgot to do during a weekend of fun, bad company and poor judgement.

Sienna Garrison never dreamed her college sweetheart, Carter, whom she pledged her life to, would break her heart and when he did, she moved out and moved on - or tried to.

What better occasion is there than a friend's wedding to stir up old feelings and memories of love, intense passion and nights of sensual titillation. Gazes from across a room after almost two years apart revealed depths of love that had never died.

Seeing Sienna again reminded Carter of what he'd lost and he vowed to never let go by doing whatever he could to get his wife back even if it included begging and pleading. Is Sienna ready to forgive and take a chance on life again with the only man she'd ever really loved?

When Carter brings on the charm and turns up the heat, no woman is immune, especially Sienna.

www.cherylbarton.net
www.amazon.com/author/cherylbarton

It's not a coincidence that casino owner, Torrence Allen, ran into his college sweetheart, Reese Michaels again; it's fate. As his memories unfold, he had tried everything to keep her in his life and his bed back then and failed at both. She wasn't ready for him then, but he hopes she is ready for him now.

Reese Michaels never thought she'd see Torrence again. Their split in college was dramatic and hurtful and still, no man had been able to win her heart. She considered herself the permanent third wheel to friends who had found love and marriage.

Their whirlwind affair, quickly turned into love just as it suddenly crashed and burned when a woman shows up to claim Torrence as hers. When it's also revealed that this woman isn't the only 'other woman', Reese finds herself left with a broken heart, shattered love and dreams of forever beyond her reach. How did she not know about the other part of Torrence's active and amorous life?

Torrence isn't ready to give up on having Reese in his life after his deceit. He finds himself in the fight of his life to finally have the love and commitment he wanted only with her. His swagger had always won women over, but it's his baggage that's causing his life to spiral out of control and he could once again find himself without the woman he has always loved.

Have you checked out book 3 of, "The Brothers of Chi-Town" series, "Claiming His Child"?

Business magnate Dexter Patterson refused to let anything keep him from checking off all of the boxes equating to achievement in life to prove that though he came from a rough childhood on the south side of Chicago, he still thrived and became a success. Looking around at those closest to him, Dexter found that he was still missing something...Love.

When aspiring model, Alyssa Kincaid met Dexter, she couldn't get enough of his sexual magnetism, fiery nights of passion, and secret rendezvous. She thought they were headed toward forever when a surprising call from him ended what they had causing her to leave Chicago, taking with her a secret.

Dexter thought that no woman could ever tame him, not even Alyssa who entranced him with her sexy body, smoky, sultry voice and untamed desire. Too little, too late, he realized he'd made a mistake by walking away and then she was gone.

Will Alyssa continue to curse kismet when Dexter suddenly reappears in her life or will she believe that his yearning for her isn't just because of their child, but because when she left Chicago, she took his heart with her?

www.cherylbarton.net
www.amazon.com/author/cherylbarton

*Don't miss book 4 of, "The Brothers of Chi-Town,"
series, "Always Bet on Black."*

Sexy, debonair, Delvin "DJ" "Black" Michaels, left Chicago as a man in search of a better life than the one he had where everyone knew him as "Black". Being fair-skinned, his nickname wasn't because of the color of his skin, but was due to his inclination to always wear the color black from head to toe.

Avalon Hart had lived her life on the edge, making due the best way she knew how even if it meant scheming men out of their hard-earned money. She learned how to survive from the streets and she was a woman who had a way with men that got her whatever she wanted, that was until she encountered DJ Michaels in Chicago, a man from her past who she had once easily swayed to her desires. She realized early that the man she encountered in New York had grown immune to her tricks, even the ones she learned how to do in bed that he loved so much.

DJ and Avalon are on a roller coaster ride to love and neither knew it. There was no telling who would end up on top, but one thing was for sure – the road to getting there was going to be filled with hot, sexy fun, a pair of handcuffs and a whole lot of sensuality that neither could resist!

www.cherylbarton.net
www.amazon.com/author/cherylbarton

Are you ready for the fire and attitude that comes with book 5 of, "The Brothers of Chi-Town" series? Come get some in "It Takes Two to Tangle"- available now.

Councilman Tucker Glass, a native of Chicago, has set his eyes on the biggest prize, that of Mayor of the city he has loved all of his life. At thirty-nine, his career spans back many years as a City Council member and then most recently, as City Council President. His resume reads like a ratings-topper novel full of accomplishments that make him more than qualified for the job, but what he wants to avoid is the drama that could block his path to the Mayor's mansion. He's always been a strait-laced politician, but his personal life could spawn a real-life reality show complete with hair pulling, tongue-lashing and accusatory finger pointing which would all occur in the first episode.

Tucker wasn't expecting his past to come back to haunt him just as he'd found the woman who was making his life complete. He would do anything to keep her in his life, but is he willing to give up his run for the Mayor's office to keep that love in-tact?

Nichelle Michaels didn't know that love could be so right until she met and fell in love with Tucker Glass, a man fourteen years older and wiser than her, but who showed her how a man should treat a woman, and that's after she spent the past year testing the water between how a man loves and how a woman loves. Now that she knows what she wants, a woman from Tucker's past could ruin her perfect love.

Tucker and Nichelle are in love, but is he willing to risk his chance at being Mayor because his ex-wife, or the woman he thought was his ex-wife, wants to now be First Lady of Chicago? Was he really ready to tangle with a woman who specialized in drama every day on television as the star on the nation's number one reality show?

Tucker may be ready for Chicago, but is Chicago ready for the drama that comes along with the popular politician?

www.cherylbarton.net

www.amazon.com/author/cherylbarton

Get the next exciting installment of "The Brothers of Chi-Town" with "Crashing into Love", book 6, available in paperback and download in 2021

Joey Kincaid was all set to finally have the life he wanted as a professional wrestler. Scouts were looking at him and thanks to a family friend, he was able to showcase his talent at monthly wrestling matches at the *Montiel Avage* Casino in Chicago. Along with his brother, Carlos, the two of them were unstoppable. Just when he thought that all if his dreams were about to come through, a car crash curtailed his dreams and he was left not knowing if would ever wrestle again.

Marlow Warren was offered the job of a lifetime as a physical therapist in New York City. After growing up in Chicago, she was ready to leave one big city to trade it in for another. As she was saying her final goodbye to the city that brought her one tragedy after another, one wrong mistake behind the wheel of her car could cost a man his life and it would be her fault. She couldn't leave Chicago after that.

Never had anyone said that a car crash was the best day of their life. Joey could say it, but then Marlow's past showed up and his life was headed for another collision and this time, he wasn't fighting for his life, he was fighting for love.

www.cherylbarton.net
www.amazon.com/author/cherylbarton

About the Author

Cheryl Barton lives in Maryland and in her spare time she loves to read espionage, crime and romance novels, cook, watch Sci-fi movies, spend time with family and friends and enjoy Maryland steamed crabs. Cheryl is celebrating 30 years as a government employee and loves writing romance novels when she's not working. Cheryl is the author of 31 romance novels, 3 inspirational novels and is proud of 4 book compilation projects with several other incredible women called, "One Sister Away: Encouraging Words from One Sister to Another" – a series of books meant to encourage, empower and inspire other women. People often ask Cheryl which book is her favorite of all of those she's written. While she finds it hard to select one favorite, Cheryl still looks to her first novel, Bachelor Not for Sale, if she had to pick a favorite because it was her first novel and the one that inspired her to continue writing.

Cheryl was a 2019 Finalist for the Emma Award given by Romance Slam Jam and a 2018 Finalist for the Literary Trailblazer of the Year award by the Indie Author Legacy Award. Cheryl is a member of the Romance Writers of America – National Chapter, the Maryland Romance Writers and the Contemporary Romance Writers groups, the Black Writers' Guild of Maryland and the International Women Writers Guild.

Indulge in more romance and inspirational novels by visiting her website at www.cherylbarton.net and connect with Cheryl on Facebook, Twitter and Instagram as @cherylbartonbooks.